FLIRTING WITH THE FASHIONISTA

CELEBRITY CORGI ROMANCES, BOOK 1

MELISSA STORM

Sweet Promise Press
PO Box 72
Brighton, MI 48116

To Michael Biscuit—
My very own non-stop barking, eating, and derping
machine

1

Ruby Ross pulled a freshly popped bag of kettle corn from the microwave and let the steam warm her face as she sucked it in the fragrant, buttery air with a contented sigh.

"Ahh, better than any spa treatment," she remarked to the fuzzy little dog squirming at her feet. She and her corgi, Diamond, had been together for almost three years now. Initially, she'd adopted the rambunctious little pup with the hopes that this new companion would help her get out into the city more—socialize, meet people.

But the tan and white corgi was far happier snuggled up on the couch than she ever was trekking through the sidewalk jungle of New York City.

Still, it didn't mean that Diamond was an easy dog to look after. She was forever demanding snacks, pets, and a four a.m. wake up time, and despite Ruby's increased exhaustion since adopting the discerning ball of fluff, she wouldn't trade her special girl for the world.

"Ready to start our party?" she asked the dog as they both made their way to the main living area of her studio apartment. Like everything else in this city, it was cramped to the max, meaning that both Ruby and her doggie roommate needed to use space efficiently and limit the number of personal items they kept. A small price to pay for being able to reside in one of the biggest fashion capitals of the world.

Diamond barked twice, then hopped up beside Ruby and attempted to swipe the popcorn bag from her hands with a quick nose and a pathetic whine.

"Stop that. You have your own." Ruby grabbed the dental bone from the drawer in the coffee table and tossed it over to Diamond.

The dog sighed and pushed the green chew onto the floor, then started on a fresh string of barks. As much as Ruby didn't like being terrorized, she knew she'd need to offer Diamond something better if she had any hope of catching the pre-show red carpet coverage.

"You're in-*corgi*-gable. You know that?" She chuckled at her own joke as she fished a bully stick from the top shelf of the kitchen cupboard and tossed it Diamond's way.

Now she was satisfied. Good.

"Okay, but no more barking. You got it? This is basically the fashion Super Bowl, and this year I actually have a horse in the race." Yeah, she knew she'd mixed her metaphors, but Ruby was far too excited about fashion and far too uninterested in sports to care either way.

This was it, the big show and her first real chance at getting noticed by the fashion bloggers, reporters, and Hollywood's most respected stars.

Time had passed in a colorful whirl ever since acclaimed director Millie Sullivan had called on Ruby to design the perfect red carpet look for this year's Academy Awards. Millie, like Ruby, wore a size sixteen and said she wouldn't trust anyone else to dress her curves right. Doing so was especially important, considering that she was up for the best director award for the first time ever—and Ruby was so proud of her for the accomplishment.

Together they'd designed the perfect floor-length red gown with a high slit up the side and meticulous beadwork along the neckline. It seemed most in the industry expected bigger girls to merely "dress for their size," concealing their figures in simple black frocks while all the skinny girls topped off the best-dressed lists.

Ruby, however, had a different philosophy.

Celebrate your body as it is, because no *body's* perfect—that's what she often said when discussing her work with potential new clients or business relations. And that's what she'd told Millie, too.

Ruby's breath caught the moment she spied her newest showstopper on the red carpet. Millie was perfection personified with a bold red lip to match the gown and a perfectly coifed 1940's updo.

"Who are you wearing?" one of the reporters called, rushing over and waving his mic in Millie's face.

Millie looked straight into the camera like the practiced pro she was. Normally, she stood behind the scenes, but tonight she stole the whole show as she smiled wide and exclaimed, "Ruby Ross!"

"Oh, I haven't heard of her before," the reporter gushed as he made a big show of examining her from top to bottom and back again. "But she does beautiful work."

"Yes, she sure does," Millie agreed, bobbing her head and showing off that bubbly personality Ruby had quickly come to love. "She's an up-and-coming force in the fashion world for sure."

"Honey, ain't nothing 'coming' about it." Turning to the camera, he added, "Ruby Ross, your star has arrived, and she looks fabulous."

Ruby screamed and stomped her feet on the floor, drawing an aggravated groan from Diamond, who was still making slow work of her prized treat. Well, not even a moody corgi could spoil her mood tonight.

"Did you hear that, girl?" she squealed. "Our whole life is about to change! Just you wait!"

Diamond picked up her bully stick and retreated to the bedroom, leaving Ruby to marvel at her good luck all by her lonesome. It didn't matter, though. All that mattered was that her work had been seen at one of the very biggest venues in the entire world. It had been noticed and then admired.

This was the big break she'd worked so hard for but had begun to doubt might actually ever come.

This was it.

And she was more than ready for whatever came next.

*B*randon Price's cell phone buzzed with an alert quickly followed by a second. Apparently he'd made the "worst dressed" list, and his father wasn't very happy about it.

Of course, he hadn't even wanted to attend the stupid awards ceremony, anyway—let alone wear a monkey suit to the thing. But when the gushing up-and-coming actress had begged him to be her date for the evening, Brandon's father had wasted no time accepting on his behalf.

That was the thing about dear old dad.

He saw his son as an extension of himself and his business rather than as his own person with his own dreams and ambitions. Price Sr.'s fitness empire had hit the big time when Brandon was still in elementary school. That meant moving to a larger, swankier house, switching to a private tutor and—worst of all—being groomed as his father's successor from a very early age.

While Brandon could appreciate the big muscles and flirtatious women that came with being heir to the popular health and fitness brand, he'd never actually gotten the chance to figure out where his own interests might lie.

And it was starting to look like he might never get the chance, either.

He'd had zero interest in the flashy awards show last night. It was so long and so boring. And besides, he'd only seen one or two of the movies that were nominated. His father had said it would be good for Brandon's image to accompany the sweet girl-next-door type to support her director who had just been nominated for the first time.

And so Brandon went, but he refused to go quietly. He'd grown a few days of messy stubble and paired his tuxedo with a mesh undershirt and neon yellow bowtie, thus achieving the worst-dressed accolade today. Not that it really mattered, anyway.

For as much as his father liked to complain about Brandon's rebellious streak, any press was good for them—yes, even the worst dressed list. For years, his bad boy image brought the fitness fanatics in droves. Everyone seemed to think that Brandon was living the perfect life filled with women, money, and fame.

Well, everyone except for Brandon himself, anyway.

Money was great, provided you could spend it on the things you wanted. Brandon's father kept close tabs on what he spent, where he went, and with whom. He wouldn't even let his son eat a slice of pizza. for crying out loud! In addition to grueling daily workouts and a regular diet of protein shakes and detox teas, Brandon wasn't allowed to eat *anything* that had been even slightly processed or that might otherwise mar his carefully maintained physique and glowing complexion.

It wasn't just frowned upon. This rule had actually made it into his contract.

It was also a condition of his trust fund, inheritance, and salary all rolled into one. Misrepresenting Body by Price would dash his wages and could possibly get him fired if he managed to take things too far.

Sometimes he'd fantasize about grabbing a super-sized value meal from McDonald's and scarfing the whole thing down right in his father's face, if only to call his bluff. And if Brandon got fired, so be it. He'd never asked for this job, and he was pretty sure his dad needed him just as much—or even more than—Brandon needed him.

Unfortunately, he wasn't actually qualified to do anything else. He'd only ever been paid to smile, look good, and parrot back all the words his father's publicity team shoved in his mouth day after day. He'd gotten his high school diploma but never had the opportunity to attend college. Dad said Brandon didn't need an education when his entire future was being handed to him on one giant organic, non-GMO platter. *Yum.*

He glanced down at his father's text now and frowned.

What were you thinking wearing that? the message came, typed out in very unnecessary all-caps.

Can't talk, Brandon texted back. *Lifting.*

That would avoid the upcoming confrontation at least for a little while longer. Give his dad some time to calm down. Despite the older man's huge success, he was always angry these days. Ever since Brandon's mom had asked for a divorce about five years ago, Dad had turned all his attention toward ensuring his son could never follow suit.

It was exhausting being the center of his dad's universe, especially since they had so little in common. It was all so shallow, every last part of the life they both lived. And Brandon longed for a way out, though he doubted he'd ever find one.

It hurt when the gossip rags called him dumb, spoiled, or any number of other insults they so enjoyed hurling his way. In truth, they didn't even know anything about him.

But then again, Brandon also knew very little

about the real him that lay hidden beneath all the glitz and glamor. He supposed the media could be right about everything. Even his father could be right what was best for him, as much as he loathed the idea.

Maybe he was just a shallow pretty boy like everyone said...

Then again, maybe he was meant to be so much more.

Brandon groaned and grabbed a heavier pair of weights from the rack. If he strained his muscles hard enough, eventually his mind would quiet down and let him enjoy the day ahead.

It was better not to think.

Just do.

Just live one day at a time.

Eventually he'd learn to be grateful for the life he had and would stop thinking about all the things he was missing... right?

2
_____

*R*uby's commissions soared after Millie Sullivan was named one of the best dressed at this year's Oscars. Within mere days, her client waiting list had filled for the year—and the orders were still coming in at an accelerated pace.

"What do you think, Diamond? Time to hire an assistant?" she asked her faithful corgi while taking a brief break to grab a protein bar and a fresh cup of coffee for lunch.

Diamond barked enthusiastically, which didn't actually tell Ruby anything considering the dog would take any and every excuse to let out a joyful noise. However, the phone rang as if it, too, wanted to celebrate their success.

"Just a sec," Ruby said, holding up an index

finger to signal the quiet command. The call had come from a number she didn't recognize, but it did have a New York area code at least. She flipped it to speaker phone and murmured a distracted "hello."

"Ruby Ross?" the older woman on the other line trilled, stretching out her name for an unnatural number of beats.

"Speaking." She shot Diamond a funny look as they both waited for the caller to declare her intentions.

"I've spent the last few days learning everything I could about you, and well... simply put, I *must* have you." The woman stopped speaking but her excited energy still seemed to pulse between them.

Ruby laughed. "My waiting list's pretty long, but I'd be happy to take your name and number for when—"

"I'm not talking one dress, dear. I want *you.*"

Ruby glanced toward Diamond and shrugged. "I'm not quite sure I follow."

Now it was the other woman who laughed good-naturedly. "I'm parked outside your building. Come down and we'll talk," she said, hanging up before Ruby could ask any further questions or argue with the somewhat off-putting request.

Alone again—well, except for the corgi—Ruby

rushed to the window and leaned forward to search the streets. Sure enough, a dark car with tinted windows sat idling at the curb below. Ruby bit her lip as she contemplated her next move. She wasn't often in the habit of getting into strange cars at even stranger people's request. Then again, she was too curious to simply ignore the invitation.

"C'mon, girl," she said at last, snapping Diamond's leash onto her collar. She had no doubt the feisty corgi would defend her, should it become necessary.

The dog barked and shifted her weight from foot to foot while she waited for Ruby to open the door. Their walks had been fewer and farther between lately, given that Ruby now needed every waking hour to make progress on her rush of new orders. She'd definitely look into hiring an assistant sometime soon, especially since it seemed this mysterious car woman had an unusually large order coming her way.

She approached the car hesitantly, not sure if the unknown caller sat in the front seat or the back. When she was just a few feet from having to make a decision, the rear window rolled down a slit, offering her a peek inside. Ruby couldn't believe her eyes.

"Lorna Stevens?" she exclaimed with a reverent

gasp. Lorna was one of the wealthiest women in the entire country. Her cosmetics and skin care line had exploded in the early nineties, and she'd been raking it in ever since.

The woman nodded and motioned for Ruby and Diamond to join her inside the private vehicle. She wore an elegant red A-line skirt that hit mid-calf and a nicely starched collared shirt with a giant string of black stones at her neck and a sparkling diamond stud in each ear. Ruby had always considered the billionairess a fashion icon. Seeing her up close now actually took her breath away.

"Thanks for coming down," Lorna said with a tight-lipped smile. "I wasn't sure if you would, but I really preferred to make my offer in person."

Ruby's heart thrummed a million miles per hour as she held Diamond tightly on her lap and stroked the dog's soft fur. "What can I do for you?" she managed despite the fact her brain had just short-circuited on her.

"Like I'd started to say on the phone," Lorna enunciated, tilting her head to the side slightly and pausing for emphasis the way she often did during televised interviews. "I want you."

"Y-y-yes," Ruby sputtered, still not believing this

exchange was really happening. "I'd love to design something stunning for you."

"Perfect." Lorna's smile grew. "How about a new retail chain of plus-sized fashion boutiques exclusively featuring your designs?"

Ruby's chin dropped to her chest. It was the only way she managed to breathe at all, keeping her mouth as wide open as possible as she gaped at her would-be patron. "Are you serious?" she whispered, almost as if saying the words any louder would somehow change their reality.

Lorna laughed. "The Body Positive movement is here to stay, and I want to do my part to empower young women of all shapes and sizes. Is that something you want, too, Ruby?"

Ruby nodded, still dumbfounded by this startling offer. It was exactly what she'd always wanted for herself but had never in her wildest dreams expected to come so soon in her career. "So much," she said with a huge smile, working hard to keep her composure in the face of this sophisticated and powerful woman.

"Wonderful," Lorna said with a quick nod. "You have my number now. That's my direct line. Do you think you can have a proposal ready for me by Friday?"

"F-F-Friday?" Ruby sputtered again. That was only four days away. Did Lorna really expect her to work out so many details in so little time?

The billionairess waved a hand dismissively. "I'm throwing a big party for *Bloom* Saturday night and I want to be able to announce our partnership then, seeing as there will be a good deal of press coverage, and I'd also like to be able to introduce you around to some of the people you need to know in this business."

"Yes. Yes, of course. I'll be ready," Ruby said, still not believing how quickly her luck had shifted. All it had taken was one little dress, one little interview, one little phone call.

"Excellent," Lorna said with another quick nod. "I'll send a driver for you at three on Friday. He'll bring you to me, and we'll take things from there. Goodbye for now, Ruby."

Ruby stumbled out of the car and stared after Lorna until she and the vehicle both disappeared into busy New York traffic.

Had that really just happened?

Diamond barked and tugged on the leash, reminding Ruby that even though her dreams all seemed to be coming true, she still lived in the real world with real responsibilities.

"C'mon, girl," she said, patting her thigh to call the dog to her. "Let's get back to work."

*B*randon was lounging on the couch trying to lose himself in some random sports game he'd found while channel surfing. Today he wouldn't leave the couch at all, not if he could help it.

Of course, only moments after making this decision, his father swept into the room and tossed a duffle bag at him. "Get dressed," Price Sr., commanded, his tone firm and inarguable. "You're going to New York."

Brandon groaned and paused the live feed on the TV. "New York? When?"

"As soon as you're dressed. I have Hector on standby." His father remained standing, staring down at Brandon as if he'd somehow offended him by trying to relax on his day off.

"Right now?" Brandon scrambled to sit up. "Then why couldn't you have told me sooner? I have a life outside of Body by Price, you know."

"If you'd stop complaining for one second, I'd tell you." The father paused and narrowed his eyes while waiting for any last complaints from his son. He continued when he saw that none were forthcoming. "There's a party, and we're one of the primary sponsors."

Brandon sighed and fell back, letting the overstuffed couch cushions catch him. "So then why don't you go?"

"We both know that's not my scene. I'm too old for stuff like that. Besides, you always get better press. Now get up and get ready."

Brandon obeyed but moved at a sluggish pace as he gathered his overnight essentials. He already had a full, separate wardrobe in their New York penthouse, which meant he probably could have gotten away with packing nothing at all for the brief trip ahead.

Even so, New York was exactly where he didn't want to be right now. He needed some down time to relax—and they called NYC the city that never sleeps for a very good reason. Even in the middle of the night, the sky in Times Square was bright as day from all the flashing signs trying to sell everything from Broadway tickets to designer underwear.

And he was so sick of being a commodity, the face of the brand, a marketing ploy more than a person. The whole thing made him want to barf.

Of course, his father had waited until the day of the party to inform Brandon that he would be attending. Probably figured his son would find a way out of it if given enough time to plot and plan. Which meant they understood each other, even though they barely tolerated one another most days.

"Celebrating healthy women both inside and out," he read from the event page and smirked. The party was being spearheaded by the women's magazine *Bloom,* a publication in which he'd often been featured, discussing tips for following the Body by Price fitness plan and even revealing what attracted him to a woman.

It was all total BS, of course.

Why did women need an unenthusiastic twenty-something male telling them how to live their best lives? He didn't even have the answer for himself, let alone anyone else. Besides, beauty was so much more than balancing your macronutrients and hitting your target heart rate for each workout session. He'd always thought of it more as an attitude. Health, too.

That's why he could always tell which of his father's newest fitness acolytes would achieve their goals and which would fail miserably. It was all in the approach, and Brandon had never believed in depriving himself of anything he wanted.

His father, on the other hand... well, he was all too happy to deprive them both.

About six hours later, their New York chauffer met him at the airport and drove them both through the slow-moving city traffic until they reached the penthouse. "Your outfit for tonight is waiting upstairs," he informed Brandon, making brief eye contact through the rear-view window. "Your stylist is waiting there as well."

"Great, thanks, man." Brandon reached forward to slap the driver on the shoulder, possibly a little too hard given the way the older man winced at his touch.

Upstairs, Brandon's stylist shaved him, lotioned him up, and tended to his hair. "Lately you've been looking a bit tired in photos. A light touch of eyeliner will brighten those eyes right back up."

Brandon balked at this and shook his head. "You want me to wear makeup? No way."

The stylist shrugged as if she didn't care either way. "Then you're all set. Have fun tonight."

"Yeah, thanks," he mumbled as he made his way back downstairs to the waiting car, feeling as his movements weren't his own and knowing that his life had stopped belonging to him long ago.

The party was in full swing by the time he arrived, the lights dark but the decorations bright and colorful. Lorna Stevens, the owner of the hosting magazine and a great deal of other similar enterprises, stood in the center of the room, everyone flocking toward her, each desperate to get some time with the generous billionairess who had launched many careers in the world of health and beauty.

Perhaps if Brandon came up with an idea for something of his own, he could pitch it to her and finally have the capital to break free of the "family business" he loathed. Of course, he had no idea what he might actually propose if given the chance.

"Oh, Brandon Price!" someone vaguely familiar shouted over the live music, then pulled Brandon in toward Lorna and her current crowd of sycophants. "Lorna was looking for you."

For him? Not sure why, seeing as he was no one special. They'd always been polite, but never friendly. So then why, of all the glamorous, successful people here tonight, had she wanted to find *him?*

He smiled somewhat nervously as he waited for Lorna to finish a side conversation.

When she finally turned his way, her eyes sparkled with warmth. She obviously had not refused her stylist's offer of an eyeliner touchup. Even beyond that, though, he could see true happiness lighting her features, and he wondered what that might feel like.

"Brandon," she said, offering him a firm handshake, the handshake that had closed hundreds, if not thousands, of business deals over the past decade. "I'd like you to meet my newest fashion superstar, Miss Ruby Ross." She let go of Brandon's hand and nudged a member of her crowd forward.

The first thing Brandon noticed about Ruby Ross was her classic red lip and the matching streak of color that darted through her otherwise dark hair. Her skin was quite pale in stark contrast to the perma-tans that flanked the streets of LA. And her gown was a stunning shimmering silver that caught and played with the light, even though there wasn't much in that dark party hall.

She looked like a second-place trophy, he thought. *Someone as stunning as her should be wearing gold.*

"I like your dress," Brandon said when he realized too much time had passed without returning

Ruby's simple, mumbled hello. Maybe it wasn't the most impressive opening line, but he had a hard time thinking straight as he followed the mesmerizing curve of Ruby's hip, first up and then down.

Oh, he shouldn't stare. He knew better. And yet...

Ruby Ross was unlike anyone he'd ever met before, and he couldn't wait to figure out why his response to her was so immediate and so intense—and whether she might be feeling the exact same way, too.

3

*R*uby had been perfectly happy to spend the evening in the company of one of the few people she already knew, racecar driver Lissa Walker.

Even though she and Lissa were just about as different as two people could come, they had two very important things in common. For starters, they'd attended the same university for their undergraduate degrees. More importantly, though, was the fact they were both owned by adorably bossy corgis. That had been enough for them to pursue the beginnings of a tentative friendship online.

And seeing as they were both unfashionably early to tonight's shindig—*oops!*—they'd decided to stick it out together, moving their Instagram friendship into the real world at last. For her part, Ruby was having a surprisingly great time, and she suspected Lissa was, too.

That is, until duty came calling in the form of a size zero redhead wearing a dress so short it looked more like a t-shirt than anything else.

"C'mon. She needs you," the young woman said, pushing Ruby toward the center of the large, open space where Lorna stood playing host for the evening.

"Are you going to be okay?" Lissa asked as she followed after Ruby and the mysterious interloper with fast, athletic strides. Her wavy brown hair had already fallen loose of the simple updo, and Ruby vowed to help her friend get ready next time they both found themselves headed toward the same party.

"Lorna's the whole reason I'm here. She wants to show me off, I guess," Ruby muttered back over her shoulder and watched as her friend stopped her pursuit.

A moment later Ruby's phone buzzed with a new message from Lissa: *Good luck!*

Ruby took a deep breath, readying herself for the networking portion of the evening. She didn't need luck because she had skill and she'd worked hard over the course of her career so far. Lorna already loved her aesthetic and had even approved Ruby's plan for the new retail chain with minimal revisions earlier that afternoon.

Ruby did briefly wonder if it had all been too easy, if she should have asked for more money, but she already felt as if the seven-figure contract was more than she ever could have dreamed.

And that was just for the first year!

She slipped through the pulsing crowd and sidled up to Lorna. "I'm here," she said, placing a gentle hand on the older woman's shoulder.

The billionairess wedged her hand in the crook of Ruby's arm and yanked her around the circle, introducing her to each new person with a glowing endorsement of all that was to come of their newly minted partnership. "This is Ruby Ross. Remember that name, because soon you're going to see it everywhere," Lorna exclaimed again and again.

Ruby smiled, nodded, shook hands, and fielded both compliments and questions about the custom-made gown she wore that evening.

"Oh, look. There's Brandon Price," Lorna said, whispering to one of her lackeys who immediately set off to fetch the newest arrival and bring him their way.

Brandon Price looked like a dream in the sharp blue suit that hugged his body like a glove. She'd seen him all over the papers and the gossip sites, most recently on the worst dressed list from this year's Academy Awards. He was a bad boy, a spoiled heir who did whatever he wanted and gave zero apologies about it.

She'd once made the mistake of trying the cleansing teas he was constantly hawking on his Instagram, and they'd made her violently ill for almost seventy-two hours until the last drop had finally drained from her system. She quickly unfollowed him after that fiasco and hadn't looked back since.

But now she was looking forward, and there he was, capturing her with his signature lop-sided grin —the same one that made women of all shapes, sizes, and ages sign away the better part of a month's pay just for the chance to take a one-hour fitness seminar with him. If others wanted to throw away their hard-earned money, that was their choice, but Ruby had grown to despise Body by Price for everything it represented.

Mostly, that they made their millions by making women like her feel inadequate. Yes, Ruby wore a size sixteen. Yes, she would prefer to wear a one-piece swimsuit if given the choice, but no—she was not unhealthy nor was she unhappy, and she was definitely not someone to be pitied.

"I like your dress," Brandon said, and she couldn't help but wonder if perhaps he was making fun of her, if he was silently completing that sentence with *I'd like it even better if it were at least ten sizes smaller.*

"Thank you," she said with a curt nod, more than ready to move on and meet the next person, but then Brandon spoke again.

"May I get you a drink, Lorna?" he said, leaning in close to both women so they could hear him easily over the crowd.

"Oh, yes. A drink would be divine," Ruby's patron cooed.

"Will you come with me?" Brandon asked, extending a hand her way.

Lorna nudged her forward, and there was no argument left to be made. She could survive a few minutes in his presence, surely.

The first thing Ruby noticed when she placed her hand in Brandon's was how strongly their complexions contrasted. He was a gold brown from all his hours spent on the beach, whereas Ruby often hid from the sun and her light, smooth skin showed just that.

The next thing she noticed was how wildly his pulse was thrumming as his fingers clasped around hers and pulled Ruby forward. He led her away from Lorna and through the crowd, not once letting go of her hand.

"Pick your poison," he said, nodding toward the pop-up bar.

Ruby shook her head. "Just a Diet Coke, please." She needed to keep her wits about her, to work on remembering each person she met and why they were important. The last thing she wanted to do was embarrass herself by becoming a sloppy drunk in public. Her deal with Lorna had come about very fast, and it could dissolve just as quickly.

Brandon laughed and made a peace sign, which he used to wave the bartender over. "Two Diet Cokes please, and a glass of your best white wine."

The bartender nodded and set to work.

"The wine's for Lorna," he said. "I've noticed she never drinks anything with any color in it. I'm sure that smile of hers is insured for at least a cool million. Probably way more."

Ruby shrugged. She'd never noticed this detail

and wondered if it was accurate. "And the Diet Coke's for you?"

"Yeah, I find it helps ingratiate me to people when I'm drinking the same thing they are." He smiled again, and her own pulse quickened despite her better instincts.

The bartender slid the three drinks their way, and Brandon handed the first tumbler to Ruby. "Here's to a night to remember," he said, clinking his glass to hers and keeping his eyes on her face as they both took polite sips.

Ruby wished she'd have ordered something stronger, but then again, no amount of alcohol could lessen the hold this gorgeous man seemed to have on her.

She needed to get away from Brandon and back to Lorna, and she needed to do it fast—or at least before his undeniable charm did irreparable damage to her self-respect.

*B*randon saw the exact moment he lost any ground he'd gained with the beautiful Ruby Ross. He'd taken things too far with that toast of his. The way her eyes darkened as she looked up at him was proof enough of that.

"Anyway…" Ruby said, glancing away from him but not yet moving in that direction. "Thanks for the drink. I can take Lorna's if you want," she added, reaching for the glass of chardonnay.

Brandon jerked it out of her reach. He had to make a bold move, and he had to make it now before he lost his chance entirely. "Nope. I'm not letting you get away until you give me your number."

Ruby's brow furrowed as she studied him disapprovingly. "Me? Why?"

"Because I want to call you," he answered truthfully, but Ruby just shook her head.

"Let's be honest here. I'm not exactly your type," she said with a frown that suggested her confidence regularly peaked and dipped depending on the subject at hand.

"What makes you say that?" he asked, widening his eyes.

"Would you like a list of sources cited?" She laughed bitterly and pushed away from the bar. "Because I'm sure it would be quite long," she said with one last look over her shoulder before charging back through the crowd.

No, Brandon wasn't ready to give up just yet. He hurried after her until he'd made up enough ground to cut her off from the front. That seemed better than grabbing hold of her wrist from behind—or at least more respectful. "C'mon, Ruby," he said, not above begging now. "The gossip mags get it right about half the time, and even that's only when they're lucky."

"So you're saying the dozens of pictures I've seen with your arm slung around one skinny blonde after another were all...what?" She huffed and folded her arms over her chest. "Faked?"

She had a point, but she still didn't understand. He needed her to understand. "Not faked, but also not completely authentic."

Ruby turned to leave in the opposite direction, but Brandon stopped her with a single word. *"Wait."*

He saw the tension drain from her as she dropped her arms and motioned toward the nearest corner. "C'mon," she instructed. "It will be easier to hear each other over there."

When they had reached the spot Ruby had indicated, she remained standing while Brandon leaned back against the wall.

"If you don't already know, you'll learn soon enough," he explained. "When you're in the public eye as much as I am, the world decides who they want you to be and they have a very hard time changing their mind once it's made up."

"So you're saying everyone's got you pegged the wrong way?" she asked, raising one well-groomed brow.

He nodded emphatically. "Not *all* wrong, but definitely some, yeah. What do they say about you?"

Ruby frowned again, and he hated seeing the way it transformed her entire face into someone almost unrecognizable. "So far they don't."

He had a hard time believing this. "Because you're so new?"

"Because when you're a bigger girl, sometimes that makes you invisible." Ruby crossed her arms defensively again. "As much as everyone talks about body positivity, taking pictures of someone like me would sell way fewer magazines."

"But you're beautiful," Brandon argued.

"Thank you for the compliment, but..." She dipped her head shyly for a moment, then raised it back up and met him eye to eye. "I've lived in this world long enough to know that change is slow to come by. I'm proud of everything I've accomplished so far, but I also know I'm going to have to work ten times harder to make a name for myself because of the types of bodies I dress. Because of the type of body I, myself, wear."

He studied her again as if seeing Ruby for the first time. She was magnificent, whether or not the rest of the world agreed. And, anyway, he suspected she was very wrong about that. How could anyone look at this gorgeous woman and not see someone worth getting to know?

Brandon almost made a comment about loving what he'd seen of her body so far but knew that Ruby wasn't that kind of girl. She'd likely find what he meant as a compliment to be at least a little—if not a lot—offensive.

She took a long, slow sip of her Diet Coke, then said, "Don't worry about me. I'm up for whatever challenge they'll throw my way."

And he believed her one hundred percent, but they still had a problem.

"The only thing I'm worried about is that you won't give me your number," he said with what he hoped was an ingratiating smile.

She laughed. "Tell you what. I'll give you my number, but you have to do something for me in return." She reached out her hand and wiggled the fingers until he unlocked his phone and handed it to her.

"What can I do for you?" he asked, practically breathless from the sudden success of this moment.

She punched in her number and handed the phone back with a triumphant smile on her face. "One of two things. Either forget you ever met me or prove that you're different."

"Different from the other guys?"

"And from what everyone says you are," she added.

"Is that all?"

"That's all." Ruby smiled in a way that suggested either outcome would be just fine by her.

But Brandon already knew which path they'd be taking, and he couldn't wait to see her again. "Then you're on," he said, keeping an eye on her as she disappeared back into the crowd of party guests.

He was more than ready to do whatever it took to spend more time with the beautiful powerhouse that had just turned his world on its head. At last things would be different.

He could already feel it.

Feel her.

*R*uby eventually found her way back to her friend Lissa, and together they passed the night quite enjoyably. A few times she found Brandon Price making eyes at her from across the room, and each time the intensity of his gaze made her blush and look away.

Brandon was incredibly handsome. She couldn't deny that.

But she still couldn't understand why he'd taken an interest in her.

Over the years, Ruby had gained much confidence since her hard days of being a bigger girl at high school, but she'd also learned to stay in her lane when it came to dating. She may not be the flashiest model, but she was nice, reliable, and attractive in her own way. Brandon, on the other hand, was like a rare, coveted sports car, the kind with doors that opened up instead of out and that only the most elite could ever dream of owning.

They didn't even belong in the same lot, let alone parked right next to each other. Couldn't he see that? Because she definitely could, and the acknowledgment made her nervous. She'd assumed she was long past the self-esteem highs and lows of her teenage years, but apparently not.

Brandon brought it all racing back.

By the time Ruby returned home to her cramped apartment, she was more than ready to take off her fancy dress and slip into a faded old t-shirt in preparation for bed.

Diamond, however, had other ideas. The little dog barked and bounced as she threw herself at the door, giving Ruby no choice but to take her out for a quick walk. She threw on her comfiest sweats and an old pair of walking shoes, then led the corgi out into the darkened city streets.

Along the way, she stopped at their favorite deli and grabbed a tuna melt for herself with a side of sliced lunch meat for Diamond. This was one thing she absolutely loved about living in the city that never slept. There were always a million things to do, and it was never too late to grab whatever late-night snack you were craving.

Diamond inhaled her roast beef and Ruby worked on her sandwich while they strolled around the city block, passing other dog-walkers as well as laughing partygoers and the tired-looking folks who worked odd shifts. By the time they made it back to their apartment again, it was practically three in the morning.

Ruby hardly had the strength to remove her shoes before falling face first into bed. She could have fallen asleep right then and there, but her phone buzzed in her pocket. making that particular task impossible for at least a little while longer.

She growled and dragged the phone to her ear. It wasn't a text or a social media notification. Someone was actually calling her at this unholy hour. She pressed the button to answer, ready to lay into whatever wrong number dialer thought now would be a good time to call anybody—let alone her.

"Hello," she mumbled, still lying face-down on her comforter.

"This isn't a booty call," a familiar male voice promised her from the other end of the line.

"What?" she asked around another yawn.

"I said, *it's not a booty call,*" he repeated with a little laugh.

"Look, I think you have the wrong number, so—"

"Ruby," the voice interrupted. "Have you forgotten meeting me already? This is Brandon Price. You gave me your number."

She forced herself into a sitting position, even though her head spun in dizzy circles from her over-long day. "It's three in the morning," she informed him groggily.

"Yeah, I was hoping to catch you before you turned in for the night. I just left the *Bloom* thing and couldn't find you to say goodbye. I didn't wake you, did I?"

She stifled another yawn and said, "No, I'm still up."

"Good." Brandon paused for a moment before continuing. "You said to forget your number or prove I'm different. I wanted you to know I chose option number two."

"Calling at 3 a.m. is not *good* different," she pointed out.

"Have breakfast with me tomorrow," he said, ignoring her barbed comment.

Ruby sighed. She didn't have the energy for this right now, and she still didn't know why he'd chosen to pursue her when there had been so many other, more beautiful people at Lorna's party. "Brandon, I'm not so sure that's a good idea."

"It's a great idea. That way I can see you before heading back to L.A. I don't know when I'll be in New York again, and I don't want to wait so long to take you out on a date."

"Why?" she asked at last.

She expected a laugh, but Brandon kept his voice perfectly level as he answered with, "Because I like you, Ruby Ross. I thought you were smarter than that."

"I am," she insisted, wondering all of a sudden what she had to prove here. "That's why I'm suspicious."

"Breakfast tomorrow. You name the place. I don't even need more than an hour of your time, if that's all you're willing to give me. Just, please."

"Fine," she said definitively, then rattled off the name of her favorite hole-in the-wall diner. "Eight o'clock?"

"See you then," Brandon said before ending their call.

Oh, she was going to be so tired tomorrow, but maybe it would all be worth it in the end. So far, she liked Brandon well enough. But she was a very busy woman, and he hadn't earned her trust yet.

Could tomorrow change everything?

$\mathcal{T}$he next morning Brandon woke up bright, early, and way before his usual time. He needed to fit in a workout both to keep up his rigorous training schedule and also to help wake himself up before grabbing breakfast with Ruby.

As he snuck in some cardio, he prepared the argument he'd use to show that he was different. He wasn't used to having to prove himself to potential dates, and that was also part of the reason he liked Ruby so much better than the usual parade of forgettable women that marched through his life.

Even though he'd played off her concerns the night before, he did actually understand where she was coming from. His father would lose his cool if he knew Brandon was interested in a body that clearly wasn't *By Price*. He wouldn't even notice the way Ruby's eyes sparkled with intelligence or the extreme talent that was reflected in the clothes she made and wore. Ruby wasn't like the waifish sycophants his father liked to surround himself with.

She was so much more, so much better.

And he sensed she knew that, too.

Which was why she was making him work to earn and keep her attention.

He arrived at the diner ten minutes early so that he could grab a table and a cup of orange juice. When Ruby arrived a short while later, she hooked her thumb in the direction of the front door. "Let's grab one of the bistro tables outside," she said, disappearing through the door without waiting for him to catch up.

The outside eating space was small, and the two little tables were pushed flush against the outside of the restaurant's cement wall. Ruby sat at the one to the right of the entrance with a happy little dog lounging at her feet.

"This is Diamond," she said by way of introduction as the animal spotted Brandon, popped to her feet, then strained against the leash to offer him a welcoming lick.

"Ruby and Diamond. Cute," he said, bending down to scratch the dog between both of its giant foxlike ears.

Ruby smiled like a proud parent. "It's not the easiest to see now, but when she was a puppy she had this distinct diamond shape on top of her head."

Brandon took a seat across from his gorgeous breakfast companion and wiped his sweaty, dog-hair covered palms on his jeans. "Thanks for meeting me today," he said, suddenly nervous. "And for introducing me to Diamond, too."

"I don't go anywhere without her," Ruby said, slipping her sunglasses from her face up into her hair. "Not if I can help it."

He glanced down at the corgi again and found Diamond sitting with her body curved and her hind legs turned out to the side while her stubby front legs stood at attention. A giant, pink tongue lolled from the side of the dog's mouth as she stared up at her own lovingly.

Brandon laughed. "I can see why."

"Do you like dogs?" she asked pointedly and then appeared to hold her breath while awaiting his answer.

"Like them, yes." He smiled to show her that he meant it, but then admitted, "Have ever owned one, no."

Her brow pinched in response. "Whoa. Why not?"

"Not allowed," he said with a shrug, wishing they didn't have to dive head-first into the deep end but no longer seeing any other choice. "There are a lot of rules I need to follow as part of my position with Body by Price. No pets is one of them."

"But that's crazy," Ruby argued. "Correct me if I'm wrong, but isn't the company owned by your family?"

He nodded sadly as he thought back to the little boy he'd been, all the tears he'd cried when his parents wouldn't let him keep the stray dog that had followed him home one day. "It is, but my dad's a stickler for routine and order. Animals can be unpredictable, and there's nothing he hates more than things being unpredictable. Thus all the rules."

Her eyes flashed with a new question. "Don't you break the rules constantly?"

"Far less than I'd like to," he mumbled.

The waitress appeared and took their orders. She also dropped a small doggie treat on the ground for Diamond, who gobbled it up in a single breath.

"Is your dad really that bad?" Ruby asked once they were alone again.

Brandon nodded and took a sip of his orange juice, not wanting to say the words aloud or to appear like an ungrateful kid riding on the coattails of his father's hard-earned success.

Suddenly, Ruby's face crumpled into a frown and

she leaned back against her chair. "Is that why you wanted to go out with me? To make him angry?"

He choked on the overly sweet liquid and had to cough to clear his throat. "Not at all, but I do like that you've made your own way, that you're doing exactly what you want to be doing."

She smirked and leaned back in. "Did you even know who I was before you met me last night?"

"No," he admitted. "But I did some research after the fact. Congrats on the new chain with Lorna, by the way."

She smiled shyly. "Thank you. But I still don't understand why you're interested in me."

"I'm not sure I understand it entirely, either." He watched her closely to make sure she knew that this wasn't a bad thing, that whatever spark had lit between them was so special to him already. "But you know what? I kind of like that."

She stared at him blankly, waiting for some kind of an explanation.

"You want to know why. Let's just say that everything else in my world is planned practically down to the minute. I'm not kidding when I say that there are a million and one rules I have to follow in order to—quote—maintain the image of Body by Price."

Ruby laughed at the goofy impression he made of his father.

"Sometimes I feel like all I am is an image," he murmured, holding her gaze to make sure she understood what he was trying to tell her.

She frowned at his admission and shook her head. "So, your idea of changing that is to reach out to someone in fashion, another industry that is literally all image?"

"But you're not like that," he quickly corrected.

"How can you say that when you don't even know me?" she challenged.

"I could tell it from the first moment I met you," he said, finally realizing what had drawn him to her. "You were in this beautiful, show-stopping dress, but it wasn't wearing you. You were wearing it."

"Generally, that's how clothes work," she said with a small smile that felt like it was just for him.

"Yeah, but that dress didn't swallow or overtake you. It just complemented who you already were. In my job as a spokesmodel, I'm basically just the living embodiment of the company. It's eclipsed anything else I might have been." He laughed and ran a hand through his hair. "Does any of that make sense?"

She studied for him a moment, trailing her

finger around the rim of her coffee cup. "It does, but why are you telling *me* this?"

"Because," he said, reaching across the small table to grab her hand and hold it in his own. "You're the first person I've met in a long time who might actually understand."

*R*uby could easily see the sincerity reflecting in Brandon's dark eyes, and it made her feel terrible. She'd treated him the exact way she always feared others would treat her. Yes, she'd judged him by his appearance—and had even almost written him off completely because of it.

"I do understand," she said, taking comfort in the heat from his touch. "It's something I've had to deal with most of my life, too."

She'd been overweight ever since middle school, and her classmates hadn't once let her forget it. The bullying had been mild and mostly harmless, but it had still left an imprint on her. Back then everyone had seen her, and most had decided they didn't like what they saw. These days few cared enough to pay her any attention at all.

That's why the deal with Lorna was truly such a huge deal. It didn't just represent an opportunity, but also a change. Now people were paying attention again, and she had one chance to make a favorable impression. Might Brandon be the key to making sure that happened?

She knew they were supposed to be on a date, and she had grown to like him now that he'd opened up and put her largest concerns at ease. But, the truth of the matter was, she didn't have time for anything but her work—and she barely had the time needed for that, either.

The waitress appeared with their orders, an egg white omelet with mushrooms for Brandon and blueberry pancakes for Ruby.

"Yours looks much better than mine," he said, raising a fork half-heartedly.

"Want to trade?" she offered, but he immediately waved her off.

"I wish, but it's another of my father's rules."

She took a quick bite, then set her fork and knife down as she swallowed. "Can you teach me the rules?" she asked, studying him for his reaction.

Diamond whined at her feet, begging for any scraps that either human might have to offer. Ruby ignored her and continued to watch Brandon as he thought about how best to answer her question.

"Why do you want to know the rules?" he asked with a heavy sigh.

Now she was the one begging him to understand. "Because I think they could help me."

Brandon dropped his fork, and it clattered against the plate noisily. "The rules make my life miserable. Why would you want that for yourself?"

"I don't want to be miserable, but I also don't want to fail." Ruby played with the napkin in her lap as she searched for the right words. "Lorna Stevens is giving me a huge opportunity and, based on last night's party, she clearly expects me to get out there and mingle as part of promoting my new retail chain. I've never been in the public eye before, not like this—"

"But I have, my whole, entire life," Brandon finished for her.

"Exactly. You know how to look and act the party, but I haven't got a clue. I keep worrying that I'll ruin everything in some stupid, amateur move. I can't do that, Brandon."

"And you want me to help you?" he asked with a frown. Did he look so dejected because she was ruining their date with business talk, or because he doubted he could do what she was asking of him?

"I'm sorry. I know you didn't ask me to breakfast looking for a job offer, but I could really use your expertise... and a friend who's been there," she added with a nervous grin. Even if Brandon received more than his fair share of negative press, she knew now that it had been fully intentional—his way of rebelling against too strict rules he'd never wanted to follow.

Brandon rapped his fingers on the table and shot her a lopsided grin. "And here I'd been wondering whether it would be too soon to kiss you after I walked you back to your door." He laughed in a self-deprecating way.

"I'm sorry I misjudged you and I'm sorry if you feel led on," she said, placing her hand in his and giving it a squeeze. "I really do like you, Brandon, but my entire life just changed at the drop of a hat. If I try pursuing this new business venture and a new relationship at the same time, both are going to fail, and fail in a big way."

He squeezed back, sending a jolt of warmth

coursing through her veins and straight to her heart. "So what you're saying is that I help you out now, and then we can revisit the whole dating thing once you're all settled in?"

"I mean, y-y-yeah, sure," she sputtered. He really wanted her and, despite being an infamous serial dater, was willing to wait until *she* was ready to give them a try. "If that's something you still want," she added softly.

Brandon smiled and let go of her hand, then immediately offered it to her again in the form of a shake. "Well then, Miss Ruby Ross," he declared with a giant grin. "It looks like I'm hired."

Diamond barked merrily—whether to agree with this turn of events or simply beg for more scraps, Ruby didn't know. She did know, however, that she really liked this sudden turn of events that meant she got to spend more time with the charming model and learn how to manage her new life in the spotlight.

As long as neither of their hearts got broken in the process, then everything would be just perfect.

*B*randon couldn't believe that his date had turned into a job interview—or that he'd been hired. This was certainly a new experience for him, and yet another way Ruby was different than all the women that had come before.

"How much longer are you in town?" she asked him between slow sips of coffee. Her lipstick left a deep red ring on the rim of her mug, but she seemed unbothered by this.

He gulped down the last of his orange juice and leaned back in his chair. "Just until tomorrow afternoon."

"Busy guy," she mumbled, smiling at him from behind her cup.

"Yeah, well, it's easier for my father and his lackeys to monitor me when we're all in the same zip code."

"I can't believe that you of all people hate your job," Ruby said with a slight shake of her head as she set her coffee down onto the table. "Every time I see your photo pop up, you look so happy."

"Follow me on Instagram, do you?" He liked that she'd chosen to follow him before they'd been formally introduced at last night's party. Perhaps that meant she'd harbored a secret crush on him as well. After all, nobody followed him for his pithy status updates or masterful use of hashtags.

She scrunched her nose up in disgust. "I did until the detox tea scandal."

Oh, that. "Definitely not one of my finer moments," he admitted. That tea made Body by Price a lot of money but had such horrible reviews it was a wonder his father had left it on the market beyond the initial roll out.

Ruby worried her lip as she trailed her finger around the rim of her mug. "Do you think I'll hate it, too?"

He waited for her to raise her eyes to meet his, then asked, "Hate what? The limelight?"

She nodded slowly, almost as if accepting a loss for a battle that hadn't even yet begun.

Letting out a soft whine, the corgi placed both of her front paws on Ruby's thigh and nuzzled the human's elbow with her nose.

Ruby sighed and reached down to scratch the corgi's neck. "It's okay, Di. I'm fine," she assured her companion.

"You're not going to hate it," Brandon promised. "Not if you're in it for the right reasons. And from everything I know so far, you will be."

"I get that I'm supposed to be the face of my

fashion line, but I thought that's what models were for." She spoke to Brandon but kept her gaze focused on Diamond. It was an odd way to hold a conversation.

"Trust me, nobody will ever care more about your company than you do. Not even Lorna. I think that's why Dad's always kept me close. Everyone likes that we've got this big family company. Makes us seem more relatable, I guess."

Ruby shifted her gaze to him, a new type of worry reflecting in her big blue eyes. "Does he know how unhappy you are?"

Brandon laughed sarcastically. "No, and I'd rather keep it that way."

"Why?" Ruby mouthed without quite saying the word aloud.

"It wouldn't do any good. At least not until I find a way out."

"Are you actively looking for a way out?"

"Not looking—more like hoping something perfect falls into my lap." He wished he had a better answer, but if she was being honest with him, then he'd do his best to return the favor.

Diamond gave up on waiting for more pets to come and dropped to all four feet, then settled back beneath the table to continue her nap.

"Now that seems like a solid life plan," Ruby teased.

Brandon let out a giant puff of air and shook his head. "Yeah, well, being rich and famous isn't necessarily all it's cracked up to be. You'll see soon enough."

"You make it sound like an affliction. Or some kind of infectious disease. Nobody's going to pity you, though. Not with all you have." Her expression was stern but not judgmental.

Brandon leaned in close to the table but resisted the urge to grab her hand again. "I don't need them to, but it would be nice if someone understood for once."

"I think I'm starting to," she said softly. "And I'm really glad I hired you now, too. I would never have guessed that you lead anything other than the perfect, charmed life. You do a great job controlling your image, and I'm ready for your magic touch when it comes to mine."

"Ruby..." He shook his head and then locked eyes with her. "I'm happy to help you out, but just remember, you actually, legitimately love what you do. That will shine through loud and clear. All you and I need to focus on is controlling your nerves and managing expectations."

She frowned for a moment, then rearranged her features into a forced grin. "I sure hope you're right," she said with a shrug. Brandon was relieved to see that the smile remained.

He joined her with a giant, lopsided grin of his own. "I'm always right. Just wait. You'll see."

*a*t first Ruby found it a bit strange sharing intimate details of her past and her hidden insecurities with a near stranger. Brandon, for his part, remained kind and mostly impartial, which made opening up easier by the day. He also insisted that they needed to understand the root cause of her fears in order to conquer them.

"Why are you afraid of speaking in front of a crowd?" he asked during their first formal coaching session, which they'd opted to conduct via video chat.

She shrugged. "I'm just better one on one, I guess. When it's just me and somebody else, I can pay attention to what they're feeling, how they react. When it's a giant crowd, it's impossible to tell."

Brandon nodded patiently, even though he obviously didn't feel the same way. "Haven't you ever heard of reading the room?"

"Heard of it, yes. Managed to do it? Not so much." She rolled her eyes and pushed Diamond off her lap so she could move around the apartment. Pacing helped whenever she got stuck on a new idea. Maybe it would also help now.

Brandon chuckled. "It gets easier the more you do it."

"So you're saying I just have to screw up really bad a few times and then I'll be a pro?" she asked with a goofy grin.

"Who says you have to screw up at all?"

"Because I'm way out of my element here." She sank back onto the couch and massaged her temples. She'd expected Brandon to offer some quick tips like a bandage, not to delve deep into her psyche.

"Don't worry. I've got you. And by the time I'm done with you, people will be coming to you for advice on how to slay the press dragon."

Now she was the one to laugh. "Oh, yeah. I'm sure."

Brandon's expression shifted into something unreadable. "Why do you doubt yourself? I mean, you seem so confident with most things. Why are you worried about this?"

"Because it's new?" she guessed aloud. Or maybe because she wanted to focus on the clothes, not all the other stuff that she now needed to do to keep up her end of the bargain with Lorna and the other investors.

"And you just assume you're going to be bad at it?" he pressed.

"Hey, I'm not paying you to offer therapy here," Ruby said at last. She tried to play it off with another silly expression, but apparently he saw right through that.

"You're not paying me at all," he reminded her with a lopsided grin. "Would it help if I shared some of my insecurities with you? Put us more on an even footing?"

She licked her lips eagerly and got up to pace the apartment again. Suddenly her lips felt very chapped. Where had she put that lip balm made from honeycomb and other organic ingredients?

"Ruby?" Brandon asked with an inquiring raise of his eyebrows.

"Oh, yes! Yes, please." How had she forgotten to answer him? Maybe it was because things were suddenly becoming too intimate, too real between them. Or maybe because she liked believing that Brandon Price was this perfect hunky hero who, for some strange reason, had decided to be interested in her.

"My biggest fear is that it's all fake," he confided in her with a somber expression. And just like that, the illusion of Brandon she'd been clinging to shattered and the real man emerged.

"What all?" she asked, knowing that something important had shifted between them—something that could never go back to the way it was before.

"My life." He frowned and let out a sigh. "I'm good at putting on a show. What if everyone else is, too? What if no one really cares about Brandon Price at the end of the day?"

"Well, this conversation took a dark turn," she quipped, hoping to lighten the mood. She hated to see him hurting like this. It was one thing for her to fear giving a bad interview, and quite another for Brandon to question everything and everyone in his life.

He let out a self-deprecating laugh. "Yeah, your fear of public speaking's got nothing on my fear of... well, everything else."

"Is that a challenge?" she asked with a playful wink.

"Maybe. What you got?" He sighed and fell heavily onto his couch, reclining comfortably as Ruby regaled him with one story from her childhood after the next.

He shared some choice memories, too, but they all seemed to blend together. He'd been put to work for his father's corporation as a child and hadn't looked back since.

"I think you win," she said a couple hours later. Now she, too, was snuggled up in her bed with Diamond at her side. Usually her business calls didn't end with an emotional tell-all, but usually Brandon Price wasn't the person on the other end of the line. She liked him more with each word he said and was still angry with herself for almost writing him off altogether.

"Maybe at this," he said with a groan. "But I'm sure you've got me beat in lots of other ways."

That was all it took to bring on another couple of hours of soul-bearing and memory-sharing. They only said goodbye when both of their phones became dangerously low on battery power.

"When's our next session?" she asked just as they were saying their goodbyes.

"I think I'm kind of sessioned out for now," he

said with an adorable laugh. "I'll text you tomorrow, though."

"Okay," she said with a smile. And everything did seem perfectly okay. In just one day, they'd tackled the deep-rooted causes of her fears, become close friends, and seen Ruby's tiny, little crush on Brandon grow into a full-fledged, all out infatuation.

Luckily, they lived more than two thousand miles apart, which meant that she was still safe from the prospect of starting an official and time-consuming romantic relationship.

Then again, they'd just spent several unplanned hours on the phone...

*B*randon rushed to grab his phone when he heard the notification chime, and a big goofy smile spread across his face when he saw who it was.

Staying out of trouble today? Ruby had texted, accenting her question with a winky face emoji.

He laughed and twisted his face into a silly expression, then snapped a selfie to send her.

Well, that's attractive! she shot back. They'd been

talking, texting, and video chatting for weeks now, but Ruby never sent him any pictures. He knew they weren't supposed to be romantically involved, but his crush had only continued to grow over the weeks.

What are you up to today? he typed.

Work, work, and more work. You?

Same.

His phone rang with an incoming video call, and Brandon clicked over without delay. "Hey, you. Looking good."

A light pink rose on her cheeks; he loved that he had that effect on her. Even though they were just friends, she never stopped him from flirting with her. And so he did plenty of it.

"You look like you just rolled out of bed," she told him with a stern expression.

"Maybe I did." He feigned a yawn that quickly broke apart in laughter. "Nah, I've been up for at least an hour. And give me a break. Time zones and all that."

Ruby's smile faltered as she bit down on her lip and mumbled, "I need your help."

"Okay. Shoot."

"Lorna has me starting this press junket thing today, and I'm kind of freaking out." She bit her lip again and widened her eyes so that they became unnaturally big like a cartoon princess. "Help!"

"Aww, want me to come out there and hold your hand?" He was only half-joking. Maybe less than that.

She laughed briefly, then arranged her features back into a scowl. "No, it will be too late by then. It starts in a couple hours, and I was worried I'd miss you before having to leave."

"Well, you've got me. And you've got this, so stop panicking."

She began pacing the length of her tiny apartment, which caused the camera feed to bounce ever so slightly with each step. Diamond barked and chased after her heels in true herding dog fashion. He couldn't see the little dog, but he knew her mannerisms well enough through Ruby to know that was exactly what she'd be doing in the moment.

"Diamond, ouch!" Ruby scolded, angling the phone so Brandon could see the naughty little creature run fast and low from one side of the apartment to the other and then back again and again.

"My dog has clearly lost her mind," she said. "And so have I. Do you have any advice to get me through?"

"Picture the audience in their underwear?" he

suggested with a lopsided grin as he began to pace himself, if only to keep the two of them company.

Ruby stopped suddenly. "Hey, none of that. I need *real* advice. What do you do when you're in front of a room full of reporters?"

"I picture them in their underwear," he quipped.

She sighed. "Brand—"

"No, I really do!"

"That's not going to work for me." She started walking again, looking even more harried now than before. "What else do you have?"

He thought about this for a moment, and with each passing second he could see her fear grow bigger and bigger. Suddenly he had an idea, and one he thought might actually work for her.

"How about you picture them wearing *your* clothes?" he suggested. "You know, the ones you designed? I guarantee they'll probably look a million times better that way, and you'll probably feel more at ease, too. At least it should remind you that you are talented and strong and have nothing to be afraid of."

"Picture them in my clothes," she said thoughtfully, stopping again as she considered this. "I think I can do that. Anything else?"

"They're just people. Remember that. Because at

the end of the day you've already impressed one of the most discerning people in all of America, and she's chosen to invest millions in you. So, who cares what some underpaid freelancer thinks?"

"Brandon, that's not very nice." Ruby's cheeks now had a pink glow from all the pacing and fretting, and it awakened her entire face in a way makeup just couldn't.

He thought about telling her how beautiful she looked in that moment but knew that wasn't what she needed from him right now. Instead, he took a deep breath and silently willed her to heed his words. "It's true, though. And you aren't being very nice to yourself, assuming things will go poorly. I don't know how many times I need to tell you you're amazing before you start believing me."

"Just one more time?" she squeaked. As usual, she was so adorable he could hardly take it. He loved how she didn't back down from showing her vulnerability, how no matter how things were going, she was always unapologetically Ruby.

"Ruby Ross, you are a dynamo, a powerhouse, a true talent," he said, taking time to emphasize each word. "Not to mention a smart and beautiful woman. Stop panicking and start living your best life."

"Okay, now you sound like one of those page-a-day calendars with the cheesy inspirational quotes."

He raised one eyebrow for the camera. "Is that a problem?"

Finally, she let out a deep, steadying breath and graced him with a smile. "Not one bit. Thanks for the pep talk. I'll call you after."

Brandon had no doubt she'd be calling soon to celebrate a successful day. Because if there was one thing he'd come to learn over the past few weeks, it was that Ruby could do anything she set her mind to.

7

*R*uby took a series of deep, measured breaths before striding onto the raised stage at the front of the long room. She still couldn't believe that all these people were here to see her. Lorna's top-tier publicity team had set everything up flawlessly, and Lorna herself promised to be at Ruby's side for the first introduction of their partnership to the general press.

Of course, Lorna's plane had gotten held up at the last possible moment, which meant Ruby would now be forced to go it alone. She could already hear the disappointed murmurings among the crowd as she looked down at them before her. They hadn't come to see her, but rather Lorna. Everything Lorna

Stevens did seemed to make the front page, whereas nobody knew anything about Ruby Ross.

Well, at least not yet. But they would.

Brandon's affirmation for Ruby ran through her mind, bringing her strength. She was a dynamo, powerhouse, true talent, and most importantly of all, he believed in her. He was one of the few people who excelled at this horse-and-pony show just as much as Lorna, and he said she could do this. He believed in her, and that meant something.

Picture them wearing your clothes, she reminded herself as she swept her eyes around the room one more time and took another step closer to the podium. There, right before her eyes, sloppy button-ups transformed into sleek blouses, boring suits took on vibrant pops of color, and ill-fitted clothing became perfectly tailored to the bodies that wore them.

"Good afternoon," she told the horde of reporters before her with a placating smile. "Unfortunately, Ms. Stevens is unable to join us today, but I am here and ready to answer your questions about our forthcoming project together."

Much to her surprise, nobody left the room following this announcement. Instead they redoubled and focused their attention solely on her. She and Brandon had practiced her elevator pitch together many times, analyzing each word choice and any possible positive or negative connotations that came with them.

She recited those words now, adding as much feeling as she could without becoming too bubbly or appearing over-rehearsed. One by one, she answered each question. A few required her to respond with "I'm not yet able to say," but she felt confident that she had knocked this horrible, scary thing right out of the park. It really wasn't so bad, and she even suspected Lorna would be proud of her.

When it was all said and done, she hailed a taxi and called Jason from its back seat.

"Well, how'd it go?" he asked, drawing out each syllable playfully.

"Amazing!" she said on the wings of a giant, relieved sigh. "Your trick worked, you life saver, you."

Brandon sounded every bit as happy as she now felt. "Hey, you did all the hard work," he insisted. "Congrats on the first of many successful press conferences."

She closed her eyes and pictured his face as they talked—the way a dimple appeared on his right cheek whenever he smiled extra wide and how his dark eyes seemed to only see her as the two of them spoke. It felt so good to have his support, to be able to call and speak with someone who understood and was rooting for her. "Tell me about your day so far," she said after they'd discussed the ins and outs of her big afternoon with the media.

"Way boring compared to yours," he said, making a dismissive sound. "What I want to know is how we're going to celebrate your big success. Any ideas?"

"I'm going to go home and get some work in," Ruby answered with a laugh, although she did briefly picture cuddling up on her couch with Brandon and Diamond to spend a quiet relaxing evening in. "There's no time to celebrate," she finished, shaking her head to erase that beautiful image of what just couldn't be. At least not yet.

"You work too hard lately. Weren't you planning to hire an assistant? What happened to that?"

She turned in her seat, so she had a better view of the street as her taxi moved slowly down it. The sidewalks were filled with people hurrying from one place to the next. She may work hard, but so did everyone else. Sometimes she worried if she stopped for even a short break, some other upstart would slide in and steal this golden opportunity right from under her. "I still am, but I've just been too busy to make the time."

"That's very chicken and egg of you." Brandon chuckled good-naturedly. "Tell me how I can help."

"Aren't you crazy busy, too, though?" Ruby had realized that Brandon always seemed to have the time for her, but she didn't think that was because he didn't put in long hours—more that he'd come to value their friendship the way she did. It served as a strong, reliable anchor keeping them steady as life rushed by from all directions.

Wind whipped by on his end of his call, leading Ruby to wonder if he'd stopped in the middle of a workout to pick up her call. "Yeah," he said thoughtfully. "But I'd rather be helping you than my dad any day of the week."

She smiled and wished for at least the hundredth time that they weren't separated by an entire country between them. Truth be told, she'd come to rely on his guidance, but even more than that, on his friendship these past few weeks. He'd done exactly what she'd asked by proving he was different, but she'd put a hold on any possibility of a relationship right from the start.

She often found herself regretting this decision now that they'd taken some time to get to know each other. Then again, her original reasoning still stood. She was far too busy to make time for a new romantic entanglement on top of all that was going on in her world.

Maybe hiring an assistant would help in more ways than one.

"Can you help me put together a job listing?" she asked, then held her breath for a moment to slow her rapidly beating heart. "That would be a huge help."

"Consider it done," Brandon answered without even a second's hesitation. "And, Ruby, I'm proud of you for the press conference, for getting some extra help where you need it, for all of it."

"Thanks," she said, smiling like a fool. And even after they said their goodbyes, Ruby continued to smile the whole way home.

*B*randon did one more quick proofread of the job listing he'd prepared for Ruby's new assistant, then saved it as an attachment and sent it over to her via email. He'd done quite a bit of research on the web, even going so far as to learn about the most common needs of a busy fashion designer, and now felt confident that he'd done a good job of helping his friend.

She called to tell him just that, not even five full minutes later. "It's perfect, Brandon," she squealed. "Thank you so much!"

"Awesome," he replied with a satisfied sigh. "Now, would you say that I saved you some time?" She always seemed so rushed these days, and he hated that she so rarely got the time to relax. Which was why he'd come up with tonight's devious plan as a way of forcing her to slow down and enjoy the evening.

The gratitude in Ruby's voice was more than apparent. "Definitely. Thank you again."

"What are you doing now?" he asked. She still had no idea about the sneak attack coming her way, but if all went according to plan, she would within mere minutes. He could hardly wait.

"Reading one of those thick business-y books Lorna's teams recommended I familiarize myself with." She flipped through the pages on the other end of the line so loud even Brandon could hear.

"Not anymore," he said, needing to free her. "Hang up and call me back on video phone, please."

When Ruby began to argue, he ended the call and waited for her to do as she'd been told.

"I can't believe you hung up on me!" she cried, wagging a finger at him as her image became clear within the screen.

He laughed and shifted his phone to reveal a table that had been set for two, complete with a fresh bouquet of roses and a chilled bottle of Zinfandel.

"Whoa," Ruby said, letting out a slow breath. "What's all that? Got a hot date tonight?"

He couldn't help but laugh. "Yeah, you."

"I don't understand. What did—?" she started, but then her apartment buzzer rang right on queue. "Brandon," she said in a stern voice. "What did you do?"

"Open the door and find out." He hoped she'd be excited and not annoyed that he'd hijacked her evening, because he couldn't wait to spend it with her.

Ruby raced down the steps to her apartment's main gate, keeping the phone with her the whole time. "Flowers!" she exclaimed, a dreamy smile breaking through. "I don't think anyone's ever sent me flowers before. Well, at least not a guy."

"Well then, I'm honored to be the first. By the way, it's the exact same arrangement as I have here," he told her, pointing his camera toward his set up once again. "Wine and food are on the way, too."

"Thank you," she told the delivery man, accepting the giant bouquet and turning back toward the building. "Thank you," she then told Brandon with something that looked like happiness sparkling in her eyes. "Although you really shouldn't have."

"Well, I didn't know how else we could have dinner together, and I hated the thought of you not celebrating your big win this afternoon."

"Brandon Price, you are too much," she said but didn't stop smiling even as she lectured him.

"Maybe," he agreed as a devilish smile spread from cheek to cheek. "But admit it, that's what you love best about me."

They both paused at the accidental use of the L-word. It was way too early for it, seeing as they weren't even actually dating. Brandon was definitely crazy about Ruby but love still felt way too big a concept. He'd often heard that you had to learn to love yourself before you could ever hope to love anyone else, and despite all his recent soul-searching, he was still coming up a bit short.

One thing he knew for sure, though, was that

Ruby Ross was the best part of his day, the best part of his life, the best part of *him*.

"You got me," she said, breaking the silence. "All that extraness is definitely one of your most endearing qualities."

"Good," he said with a nod. "Now get everything situated on your end, because the food should be there any minute and I'm starving."

"You take such good care of me," she said as she set the roses in the center of her table. "What did I do to deserve such a great friend?"

He knew she meant that question rhetorically, but he still couldn't help but answer, anyway. "I ask myself that same thing every day," he said with a serene smile. "Ever feel like sometimes people come into your life for a very specific reason?"

"Like Lorna?" she asked with a small chuckle.

"And me," he added.

"Yes," she whispered. "I think about that every time we talk. I'm a lucky, lucky girl."

And he was the luckiest man alive.

8

*R*uby's apartment door buzzed for the second time within the span of less than ten minutes.

"Finally!" Brandon said with a dramatic sigh. "He should have been there at least five minutes ago."

Ruby chuckled and went to collect her dinner from the food delivery service outside. Even before she opened the plastic containers, the smell of fresh basil, oregano, and a heavy cream sauce practically put her into a food coma.

"Spinach alfredo," she cried once she unpacked everything onto her tiny kitchen table. "How did you know it's my favorite?"

"I know a lot about you, Ruby," he said, watching

as her eyes grew wide. "Mostly because you told me your whole life story a few weeks back. Remember that?"

She blushed, the perfect complement to the roses that adorned each of their tables. "I really did tell you everything," she said with a nervous little giggle.

"Yes, you did. That's why I know that spinach alfredo is your favorite because it's the meal you were eating when you found out you got accepted to your dream internship in the city. You said that was the start of everything, remember?"

She nodded, a mischievous smile playing at the corners of her lips. "I do. And I also know that your favorite dinner is a nice New York strip served medium rare with grilled zucchini instead of potatoes because your father doesn't allow starchy carbs. Is that what you're having tonight?"

"Nope," he said, puckering his lips so the *P* sound really popped. "I'm joining you for some good old-fashioned alfredo."

She laughed uproariously. "Your father is going to kill you," she said between gasps for air.

"Then at least I'll die happy," he said with a flirtatious wink. He wanted to have this meal with Ruby, and it didn't feel right ordering something different for himself. "You ready to dig in?"

She used her pop socket to angle her phone on the table so that she could use her hands to eat, while Brandon did the same.

"Oh, before I forget!" he cried, angry with himself for almost blowing this part of the surprise. "Did Diamond get the little dinner treat I sent for her, too?"

Ruby bit her lip as she searched through the boxes on her table. "Is that what this giant hunk of grilled chicken is for?"

Uh oh. "Did they not cut it up?"

"They didn't need to," Ruby answered with a laugh. "She'll inhale it in a single breath, anyway. Watch."

She called to her corgi, and the little dog sprinted out from under the table and began to spin in excited circles before her. Ruby picked up her phone again so Brandon could watch, too, then tossed the chicken breast to Diamond who, sure enough, gobbled it down in one grateful chomp.

"Wow, you need to enroll that dog in an eating contest," Brandon joked. "She clearly has a talent she needs to share with the world."

"Yeah, her and every other corgi on the planet."

Ruby laughed again, and it felt great after the long, busy day she'd had.

Brandon spun his fork in the noodles preparing a big, creamy bite, while Ruby did the same. They both raised their generous bites toward the screen in a quick toast and then took that first, precious mouthful at the exact same time.

Brandon let out a sexy moan. "I think I've died and gone to Italy."

"Little Italy, at least," she said. "We'll have to go there together the next time you're in New York."

"Ruby Ross, you've got yourself a date," he said, and she didn't find it necessary to correct him. Maybe by then she would be ready to turn a new romantic leaf in their relationship. She definitely loved having Brandon in her life and wanted to make sure she'd have him for a long time to come.

Keeping a guy in the friend zone indefinitely never worked out well for anyone involved in such a fiasco. Besides, kissing those full, smiling lips would be like a dream come true.

It figured. All her career dreams were already becoming a reality, so of course now she'd replaced them with her longing for Brandon, that he could one day become more than a friend.

Truth be told, he already was.

"*I* need you to put in an appearance at Body Con," Brandon's father said the moment his son picked up the phone. "It's in New York this year, and before you say—"

"Yes, I'll do it," Brandon answered, cutting his father off mid-argument. "Next week, right?"

"Well, all right, then. Thanks."

They said a quick goodbye, and Brandon went about planning a surprise for Ruby. He hadn't seen her in person for about a month, not since that breakfast they'd shared the morning after the party. He'd wanted to fly out and see her since, but it hadn't seemed appropriate given they were just friends and colleagues.

Now he had the perfect excuse.

He'd been laying low the past several weeks, only going where his father sent him and making sure to avoid photos with any past girlfriends or other women who the media had dubbed "his type." The last thing he wanted was to make Ruby think his interest in her wasn't serious or could easily be brushed aside.

Granted, that was easier said than done, but he liked the challenge.

All the extra time he'd saved from skipping recreational parties also allowed him to do some soul-searching. If he really wanted to leave his father's company, then he needed to come up with a viable plan for doing so. He'd need to find some kind of job to help pay his own way in life, and that was the tough part.

Sure, he could always approach one of Body by Price's chief competitors and offer to be a spokesmodel for them instead. They'd jump at any chance to discredit the biggest player in the industry. But even though Brandon hated working for his father, he still loved his dad and didn't want to do anything that would hurt him—at least not any more than his reaction whenever Brandon finally got around to saying those two little words that had been at the tip of his tongue for years. *I quit.*

Until he came up with the perfect solution to all of this, it was easier for him to spend his time texting and chatting with Ruby and daydreaming about what it would be like to take her out a date.

This impromptu trip to New York offered him his first chance to make this happen, and he wanted to plan something amazing.

Brandon had often asked himself why he'd chosen Ruby Ross of all women to become infatuated with. Was it that she was the right person for him, or that this was the right time for him to start looking for something a bit more serious in life? Maybe both were true.

True, she wasn't his usual type—and maybe that was the point. She represented something different, a new era of Brandon Price. Perhaps it was because everyone expected him to act a certain way, do certain things, and he was just plain tired of conforming to their expectations.

Most of all, though, he knew it was because he admired her. She'd fought her way to the top of her field with raw talent, no nepotism required.

He'd been coaching her on how to handle her newfound fame for weeks at this point, but what he really needed was for her to teach him how she'd done it. Hadn't she been afraid? Scratch that—hadn't she been absolutely terrified?

Because he *still* was.

Did she learn to ignore that fear, or did she instead choose to harness it? And how was she able to walk away from all the other great possibilities in life so that she could doggedly pursue that one thing she wanted more than anything else?

He admired her for saying no to a relationship right now. He also hated being forced to wait but liked that they'd been able to form such a solid friendship in the meantime.

That's why planning a day out with her was such a difficult task. There were hundreds of things he wanted to do with her, and he hated that they'd be constrained by any kind of time limit on his short visit.

Honestly, he'd be perfectly happy heading back to that tiny diner for breakfast. He liked the everyday simplicity of it and didn't feel like he needed flashy parties or expensive price tags to keep her happy. That was another way she was so very different from all the women he'd crushed on before. She'd always been different—*better*—but she'd also come so far in the short while he'd known her.

Brandon thought back to their first meeting at the *Bloom* party, how she'd preferred to hang close to her friend rather than mingle. And now hardly thirty days later, she was handling press conferences all on her own with zero backup.

He was proud of her, and he wanted her to be proud of him, too. But he just wasn't ready yet. Yes, he'd been searching his soul for weeks now, but so far he hadn't found any of the answers he'd been looking for.

What would Ruby do? he found himself wondering. She'd probably discovered her love for fashion design in preschool and spent every moment of her childhood working toward where she was now. Brandon felt embarrassed that he was already in his late twenties and didn't yet know what he wanted from life.

Well, except for one thing.

Ruby.

9

A few days later, Ruby posted flyers for her job listing around all the fashion colleges and institutes within a five-mile radius of her apartment, hoping that this tactic would yield better results than a generic online call for applicants.

By the end of the week, she'd selected five resumes for follow-up and sent the other dozen or so straight to the trash. Fortunately, she managed to arrange all her interviews for the same day, which meant that with any luck she'd have her decision made by the time she headed to bed that evening.

Ready to get things started, she parked herself at one of the little tables outside her favorite diner, with Diamond in tow. The little dog typically had a good read on people, and any potential assistant of hers would need to be okay with hanging around Diamond for most of the workday, seeing as Ruby still worked mainly out of her apartment.

Ruby ordered a coffee for herself and set down a bowl of water for her dog while she waited for her first interviewee to arrive. She'd be sure to leave an extra generous tip for the waitress in exchange for tying up one of her tables for a few solid hours.

Her first appointment, Heather Clark, arrived five minutes late. Ruby tried not to hold that against her, given the unpredictable nature of city traffic, but still felt more than a little irritated. The girl was thin, beautiful, and hardly a day over eighteen, by the looks of her. Her handshake was firm as she looked Ruby right in the eyes and said hello without any apology for her tardiness. And while Heather's application had looked fantastic on paper, her know-it-all attitude made Ruby very nervous. Definitely not a trait one wanted in an assistant.

The next interviewee was on time, but also allergic to dogs. On the phone she'd assured Ruby this "minor allergy" wouldn't be a problem, but then she sneezed at least fifteen times during their half-hour interview, which led both women to agree the job just wouldn't be for her.

Applicant number three knew nothing about

fashion and admitted he'd padded his resume to get the interview because it was so conveniently close to his apartment. That was a hard pass for Ruby.

Number four was summarily dismissed by Diamond, who took an instant and intense dislike to the bubbly young woman.

That left the fifth and final interview, which Ruby prayed would go better than the first four had. Otherwise she'd have to start this whole time-consuming process all over again, and she'd barely managed to make time for this first round.

Much to her relief, Shasta Jones arrived on time and had even brought a small gift for Ruby, a bracelet she'd designed herself using a skillful blend of wire and beadwork.

"I love it," Ruby cried, immediately slipping it onto her wrist. A perfect fit. "Thank you so much!"

The rest of the interview proceeded just as nicely, with wonderful Shasta giving one perfect answer after the next. By the time their half hour together came to an end, Ruby knew this was the one she wanted to hire. She made the offer then and there, and Shasta gratefully accepted. They both agreed she would start the following Monday at eight.

Well, maybe that hadn't been so hard, after all.

Ruby floated back to her apartment on a happy little cloud—glad everything had worked out despite that initial string of horrible interviews. The very moment they rounded the stairs to her third-floor apartment, Diamond began to bark for joy and pull hard against her leash. Ruby spotted the reason why a short moment later.

"Brandon, what are you doing here?" she exclaimed, rushing down the hallway toward her friend, who sat waiting outside her door. "I had no idea you were coming!"

He pushed himself to his feet and gave her a tight, lingering hug. Even though most of their friendship had been remote and they'd never actually made physical contact like this before, his embrace felt warm, familiar.

She also wasn't quite ready for it when he let go and pulled away.

Brandon's smile was gigantic as he took her in. "Surprise!" he cried, hugging her a second time, then staying close as they talked. "I have an engagement in the city and thought I'd stop in early so the two of us can hang out a bit."

Ruby's heart fluttered in her chest. Did this mean he still had feelings for her? Or had they transitioned firmly into the oft-dreaded friend zone by now? And why had her breath become labored as she stared up at the gorgeous man she'd begun to know quite well?

"Sounds fun," she managed at last. "What did you have in mind?"

Never in a million years could she have guessed that the same man who'd once sold her that questionable detox tea would become someone whose approval and admiration she craved above all else.

Sometimes life was cruel. Sometimes it was hard. But sometimes it was so wonderfully unexpected that she just had to stop and appreciate the randomness of it all.

Brandon was handsome, fit, and practically born famous, while she was plain, curvy, and had to work hard for every scrap of success she'd managed to land so far. And yet...

Their differences made their budding relationship that much more special. Ruby now knew she could count on Brandon to offer a fresh take whenever she needed one. He approached life differently than she ever had, but that made every conversation with him that much more exciting, too.

And as she opened up her apartment and welcomed him inside, she couldn't help but notice how much she liked the look of him there among all her things. How if she wasn't careful, she'd never want him to leave...

*B*randon had agonized long and hard over where to take Ruby during his surprise visit to New York. He'd considered all the grandest, most romantic locations as well as all the wackiest, most out-there options. In the end, he decided that simple would be best. That way they could just enjoy being together without any major distractions to direct their attention elsewhere.

"An afternoon in Central Park? Wow. Does it get any more cliché than that?" Ruby teased when Brandon had delivered the two of them plus Diamond to the location via his driver. She continued to laugh good-naturedly as they made their way toward the famed Bethesda Fountain and Terrace.

Brandon shrugged as they walked past a bridal party setting up for photos. "Hey, it's cliché for a reason."

"You've got me there," she admitted, and now that they were together in person, he so badly wanted to reach out and take her hand, to wedge his fingers between each of hers and feel her heart beat a tattoo against his skin.

Yes, he wanted to, but he also knew it wouldn't be right. She'd asked him to wait, and so that's exactly what he would do. Not the easiest task, given he'd called off dating altogether during these precious weeks of getting to know Ruby.

"Let's get some ice cream," he suggested, spying an umbrella-topped cart down the walkway. He could sure use a way to cool down—something to keep his hands occupied, too.

Diamond barked her agreement.

"Isn't ice cream, you know, against the rules?" she asked with a knowing wink.

Okay, that was it. He couldn't resist looping an arm over her shoulders as they strolled slowly side by side. "You're not the only one who's been learning new things this past month. I'm picking stuff up from you, too."

She twisted beneath his arm and gaped up at him in mock horror. "Oh, no! You're not blaming this one on me. Have the ice cream or don't, but you need to take full responsibility for whatever you decide."

And then she picked up his arm and draped it across her shoulders again, snuggling in close to his side. Did that mean she enjoyed touching him, too?

That she might let him hold her hand or even kiss her before the day was through? It had been such a long time since Brandon fantasized about holding a woman's hand, since he'd agonized over a kiss rather than just going for it.

"For the record, I think you should go for it," Ruby said, and it took him a few seconds to realize she meant the ice cream. "Life is too short not to be able to appreciate the small things."

"Just for that, I think I'll get a triple scoop." He quickened their pace, excited for this small act of defiance even more than for the taste of the sweet treat he hadn't been able to properly enjoy for years.

A few minutes later, they were seated at the fountain with giant ice cream cones for each of them and a pup cup for Diamond.

"That was way too easy," he said, dragging his tongue around the stacked cone in a slow, languorous circle.

"Of course it was easy. It's ice cream, not nuclear war."

They both chuckled and Brandon edged closer to Ruby until their hips were touching.

Ruby licked a splotch of melting chocolate from her lip and glanced up at him through veiled lashes.

"It's a nice day," she mumbled, keeping her eyes glued to his mouth.

"It's the best day," he agreed in a breathy whisper, lowering his gaze as well.

"We should..." Her words trailed away as he finally covered her hand with his. An intoxicating warmth passed between them, and Brandon had to fight hard not to lean in and take the kiss he'd been fixated on all month. He wanted her to make this decision, needed to know it was okay.

"What should we do?" he murmured as a spring breeze swept across the terrace and lifted strands of Ruby's hair in an unexpected dance.

She placed a hand on his chest, and his heart thumped wildly in response.

Feeling emboldened now, Brandon let go of Ruby's hand and ran both of his up her arms until they came to rest on either side of her neck. So soft, so inviting. Not like any of the women he'd been close to before. Ruby commanded her space. She didn't apologize for her body, like so many thinner women did, and this made her absolutely irresistible to him.

He let out a small whimper. It was so hard not to kiss her. He so badly wanted to find out how her lips felt, what her mouth tasted like underneath all that delectable chocolate ice cream.

"Brandon," she said softly, almost like a promise.

"Ruby," he repeated, edging his hands up to cup her jaw.

She sucked in a deep breath and then slowly lowered her lashes. The invitation had finally been issued. He tangled one hand in her long dark hair and kept the other touching her face as he leaned in and pressed his lips to hers.

The sweet serenity of that perfect moment didn't last long, however, because a jealous barking dog hurled herself between them.

"Diamond!" Ruby said through a fresh, bubbly laughter. "Down, girl!"

Brandon laughed, too, because he had no doubt that he'd soon find another chance to kiss his dream girl yet again.

10

*R*uby giggled as Diamond covered her with frantic, sloppy kisses.

"Uh oh. Looks like I've got some competition," Brandon joked before letting out a happy sigh.

She reached over to scratch her dog between those oversized ears she adored and smiled at Brandon shyly. She'd told him she didn't want a romantic relationship when they first became friends, but she'd also changed her mind in the time since. And their kiss, while brief, had been just as perfect as she'd often imagined it would be.

Maybe it wouldn't be so bad, finding a way to balance work and love. And even if it proved difficult, at least it would be worth it.

Love.

Could that really be in the cards for her someday soon?

She'd certainly come to value Brandon as a friend. What would things look like between them now that they've shared the first of what she hoped would be many more kisses to come?

Brandon cleared his throat, then laced his fingers in hers. "I hope that was okay. What I did." He studied her hesitantly, as if waiting for something to go wrong. No, everything was very much right.

"It was more than okay," she assured him with an awkward nod.

His smile grew as he shifted his focus to Diamond. "I don't think our doggie chaperone would agree with you."

Ruby glanced down and saw that her usually carefree corgi was now standing guard with her full attention pointed directly at Brandon. "Oh, she's just not used to things like that happening," she admitted with a laugh. Truth be told, neither was she. "Besides, it's in her nature to herd. Maybe she thought you got too close and had to put you back in your place."

"Back in my place, huh?" He raised both eyebrows in question. "Well, what do you think about that?" He seemed even more nervous than she felt, and that realization made her fall even harder for him.

She gave his hand a squeeze to show him she meant what she said. "For once, I disagree with her. Sorry, Di."

Brandon leaned in and kissed her cheek, which immediately upset the corgi again. "Oh, relax!" he said, tossing a smile the little dog's way.

Warmth lingered from where Brandon's lips had pressed against her skin, but soon that pleasant sensation became unbearably hot. She glanced past him and noticed a couple of women staring straight at her with intense, probing looks on their faces. When she swept her vision further around the terrace, Ruby found even more people observing her and Brandon.

"I think we're being watched," she mumbled, giving his hand a squeeze, this time because she felt afraid.

"Well, yeah. You happen to be *the* brightest rising star in fashion. Of course we're being watched." He raised their joined hand and kissed the back of hers, completely unbothered by the fact that their tender moment had an audience.

"I don't think that's why they're looking," she confided in him with a frown.

"Don't worry about them," Brandon said as he stood, then also helped to pull Ruby onto her feet.

They held hands as they strolled around Central Park for the next couple hours. Brandon didn't seem to have a care in the world. Ruby, however, became increasingly aware of strangers' eyes on them. Was this what Brandon lived with every day? You'd think there would be enough famous people in New York that the two of them could enjoy a leisurely walk around the park without having their every move scrutinized.

It wasn't until Brandon delivered Ruby and Diamond back to their apartment that he became notably agitated.

"I wish we had more time," he groaned, making a fist at his side. "I have a meeting across town and am probably already late. I'm still not ready to say good-bye, though."

"Come back after," she said, leaning back against the door and hoping he'd at least make the time to kiss her again before heading off for his work obligation. "We can have a late dinner together."

"*Mmm,* think I'll do just that." He hummed a beat, then placed one hand against the door and wound the other in Ruby's hair.

"Wait!" she cried just before his lips met hers.

Working the knob behind her, she fumbled with the door until it opened just enough to nudge their discerning chaperone through the door.

Once Diamond realized what had happened, she barked in protest, which made them both chuckle. They still stood so close that she could feel his warm breath on her forehead.

"Okay," she said, smiling up at Brandon, eager for a full first kiss between them.

He leaned in even closer and touched his lips to her forehead, a tender gesture built from the many hours they'd spend talking, texting, and getting to know each other. In some ways, today had been their first date. In others, they were starting their new relationship already very deep in. Perhaps that should have terrified Ruby, but it didn't.

Not with Brandon.

He lifted his mouth from her forehead and brought it down to join hers—slow, sweet, but also full of need. This was where he belonged. With her. No matter how mismatched they might seem. They fit together in a way Ruby had never experienced before.

Did Brandon feel it, too?

His tender expression seemed to suggest that he

did. As much as she loved staring into his handsome face, she wished he'd kiss her again. Still. More.

"I'll be back as soon as I can," Brandon promised, keeping his eyes on her as he walked backward down the hall.

Ruby couldn't wait.

*B*randon hated leaving Ruby again so soon, but he loved knowing that he'd be right back in her arms the second his work meeting ended. Never had he been so eager to clock out for the day as he was that night.

He smiled, made small talk, and batted compliments around exactly as he'd been taught. Once the investors seemed satisfied with his performance, he bolted out of that five-star restaurant as fast as he could without actually breaking into a sprint, then hailed a cab rather than waiting on his driver to appear. Ecstatic to be heading back to her, he fired a quick text to Ruby so that she would know he would be with her soon.

As soon as he unlocked his phone, a series of notifications flooded the screen. Apparently, he'd missed several calls, texts, and voice mails from his father over the past few hours. *Uh oh.* It had to be serious if his father had taken it upon himself to leave not just one, but three voicemails. He pushed the button to return his father's call, praying that whatever the issue was it wouldn't take away from his forthcoming evening with Ruby.

Brandon sucked in a deep, shaky breath when his father picked up on the first ring. Also not a good sign.

"Brandon," his dad shouted into the speaker. "What were you thinking?"

"Hang on. I just got out of the meeting you scheduled for me. It went well, by the way." He lowered the volume several notches, so that the conversation would remain at least semi-private.

"I don't care about that," his father grumbled dismissively. "I want to know why you're suddenly trying so hard to undermine our business."

Undermine? What? Did this mean he knew about Brandon's soul-searching? About the fact he wanted to leave Body by Price—and soon?

"I don't know what you're talking about," Brandon said, watching the traffic lights glow bright on either side of him. The driver studied him through the rearview mirror, and Brandon offered him an apologetic shrug.

"It was one thing when you were going through women like a Pez dispenser, but this... this takes the whole cake. Probably ate it, too."

Women? He did not like the direction this conversation was heading. Better to play stupid than to give his father information he didn't already have. What he had with Ruby was still too new, too special to be torn apart from his judgmental dad.

"Again, I'm not following," Brandon said with a sigh. "So either explain it to me or leave me alone."

His father didn't waste a second. "The paps were all over you this afternoon," he hissed through the phone. "There's at least a couple dozen shots of you making out with some heifer in Central Park."

"Wait, are you talking about Ruby?" Brandon's heart sank. If his father was this angry over a mostly innocent afternoon spent in the company of a beautiful woman, then chances were good that the online community didn't have many nice things to say either. Chances were also good that Ruby would see —or had already seen—those undoubtedly terrible things, too.

His father scoffed. "So it has a name? Have you even stopped to think how much you could hurt that poor girl by using her like this?"

"*It?*" Brandon raged, not caring anymore that the

cab driver's eyes were glued to him rather than the traffic ahead. "Are you really so stuck-up that you think someone being bigger make them less of a person? And has it ever occurred to you that I may really like her?"

"Oh, Brandon, please. We both know you're as shallow as they come. You can get much hotter women, models and actresses even, so don't act like you're slumming it for any other reason than to hurt me and the business."

"You're disgusting," Brandon ground out through clenched teeth.

"No, you are. I saw the pictures of you stuffing your face with chemical-laden street food, too. I want you to skip Body Con and come straight home. We have a lot to talk about, and I don't think it can wait."

"I'm all too happy to skip Body Con, but I'm not coming home."

"Watch it, or you won't have a home to return to."

"Fine by me." Brandon slammed the phone down on the worn bench seat, still fuming. Had he just quit his job at Body by Price? He wasn't exactly sure, but he also knew he didn't care about that.

All that mattered now was getting to Ruby, to make sure she understood that he'd never wanted any of this attention. That whatever they were saying about her, about him, it wasn't the slightest bit true.

He was crazy about her, all of her, and he hated that his father couldn't even fathom the idea of him falling for someone who wore slightly larger clothes. Maybe he'd been shallow like that before, too, but it didn't mean he had to stay that way.

Ruby had changed him in so many wonderful ways, and he refused to go back to the way things had been before.

Oh, how he hoped she'd give him the chance to explain.

That this first bad experience with the savage Internet gossip didn't destroy the beautiful new relationship they'd begun to build together.

He should have prepared her for this—for them.

Should have waited until they had a moment alone before he tried to kiss her. Should have protected her every step of the way rather than only focusing on what he wanted in each moment.

This was all his fault.

11

*R*uby's phone pinged with an incoming text. Ooh, did that mean Brandon was finally on his way? She'd missed him these past few hours. It was hard knowing he was in the same city but busy with something else.

Her smile faltered when she saw the message had, in fact, come from her friend Lissa: *Have you seen this?*

The link to an article came through next, and Ruby opened it up, expecting a funny meme or cute corgi video. Instead, she was confronted with a very unflattering photo of herself as she walked hand in hand with Brandon while shoving a towering cone of chocolate ice cream into her face.

She'd always known the handsome model was

out of her league but seeing them right next to each other like this really drove this painful point home. The angle of the photo gave her a double chin and spotlighted her notable lack of thigh gap or flat tummy. Brandon, however, looked just as fit and perfect as he always did.

Closing her eyes for a second, she tried to calm her nerves before turning her attention to the text of the article.

Is this the new Body by Price? the headline read. The text beneath boldly claimed: *Because if so, we'll pass.*

No, no, no, no! Ruby's reeling brain screamed. What had she been thinking, getting involved with someone like Brandon? Did it really matter that she was crazy about him, given that everywhere they went people stared and judged? She knew she hadn't imagined the gawkers at Central Park. She may have been paranoid, but it had obviously been with good reason.

Ruby sucked in a deep breath, then continued on to the rest of the article:

Brandon Price, the face of his father's company Body by Price, was spotted today in Central Park cozying up to new plus-size fashion designer, Ruby Ross, in a pairing that, quite frankly, has us scratching our heads.

Brandon's entire career has been made on convincing women to turn over their hard-earned dollars for over-priced detox supplements and under-effective fitness methods. And while new to the scene, Ruby Ross snagged a slick deal with Lorna Stevens for celebrating body positivity and empowering women of all sizes to enjoy dressing their bodies. *That last part is a direct quote from Ms. Ross's website, by the way.*

So, which of them is full of it?

Has she hired him to help melt the pounds away, or has he secretly harbored a fat fetish this whole time?

These pictures would suggest the latter, given the sinfully oversized ice cream cones and even more distasteful kisses they shared at Bethesda Fountain in Central Park earlier this afternoon.

I smell a scandal brewing, and I'll bet it tastes much better than Price's signature blend of diarrhea-inducing detox tea.

Ruby read the article again and then proceeded to torture herself by reading it a third time, too. Would this have even been news were she a few dress sizes smaller? She doubted it.

She didn't doubt, though, that Brandon's father would be absolutely furious about the negative press their dalliance had brought to his company. Hopefully Lorna would be more understanding. Could that sweet kiss she'd shared with Brandon in the park prove to be the kiss of death for her infant career?

She liked Brandon, liked what they'd started to build—but it was so much easier for them to walk away from their new relationship than from everything else they'd already worked so hard to gain in their careers.

As much as she didn't want to, Ruby knew she'd need to say goodbye—for both their goods.

And that's exactly why, when Brandon appeared at the apartment a couple hours later, she refused to open the door.

"Please, Ruby," he begged through the tinny speaker. "Will you let me up to talk this through?"

"I don't think that's such a good idea," she said, her finger shaking as she pushed the button to transport her voice to the speaker three floors down.

She heard him growl and resisted the urge to glance out the window to see if she could catch a glimpse of him. His voice rose up to her once again, "They say bad things about me all the time. I don't care." He said each word slowly, emphatically, and she knew he was hurting, too.

"But I do," Ruby said, fighting back tears. As hard as it was to see bad things written about herself, she hated even more that Brandon's business ethics had been called into question simply by associating with her. She couldn't have that guilt hanging over her head.

Brandon's voice came out pained. "Then I guess I'll go. Goodbye, Ruby."

And as hard as it was, she didn't try to stop him, but she did push the curtains aside to watch as he walked away from her building and out of her life. Her first instincts had been right. She never should have gotten involved with Brandon Price. Now she knew what she was missing, what she was giving up.

And it was a hurt she knew wouldn't be going away anytime soon.

Diamond came over and plopped down beside her, staring up at Ruby with her tongue lolling from the side of her mouth as she panted gently.

She didn't have a boyfriend, but she still had her best fur friend forever. And that was something.

*T*he very first action Brandon took while skulking away from Ruby's apartment was to send a text to his mom: *Quit on Dad. Can I move in with you?*

It would probably take her a few hours before she actually checked her messages, but at least he had no doubt that she would agree to help him out. And just like that, Brandon realized just how pathetic he'd become, how pathetic he'd always been. Now he'd been rejected by the first woman he'd cared about in a very long time and was also without a job or any savings to speak of. Seeing as he'd officially been dumped by Ruby, he supposed he could go crawling back to his father.

But considering the way his dad had spoken about Ruby...

Even if Ruby was out of his life for good, Brandon knew he could never forgive his father for the horrible things he'd said. *Never.*

As a young boy, Brandon had often wished that he would one day grow up to be just like his dad, his hero. Now he wanted nothing to do with the man who viewed other people as less than human just because they didn't fit his stingy criteria for determining worth.

Had Brandon unwittingly made people feel like that, too?

It was possible, and he hated that about himself. He'd been so blinded by his narrow view of success that he'd practically forgotten that there was another world out there. Maybe that was why he'd become so unhappy in recent months. Even before meeting and falling for Ruby, he'd known something was wrong, missing.

Now he had even less than before, but at least he had his dignity. That at least had to count for something.

Drifting through the city he'd visited often but never called home made him feel as if he were still connected to the greater world. Yet again, he was wandering aimlessly with no true destination in mind. Story of his life.

His phone rang just as he was debating throwing complete caution to the wind and slipping into the pizzeria for a gigantic, greasy dollar slice. He was a free man. The rules no longer applied.

"Brandon," his mom's voice came out rushed and a bit breathless. "What happened with your dad?"

"Let's just say he showed his true colors and I realized I didn't much care for them." He quickened his pace, the pizza place forgotten as he raked a hand through his hair. Only hours ago, he'd threaded that same hand through Ruby's gorgeous locks. What an awful turn this day had taken. He'd wanted to surprise Ruby, but instead he'd spoiled everything.

His mom paused, and he could just imagine her working hard to say something nice about Brandon's father. As much as she hated her ex, his mother had always been careful when speaking of her son's father. He liked that about her.

"You know your father loves you more than anything. Don't you?" she squeaked at last.

"No," Brandon corrected with a groan. "He loves himself and that stupid business of his."

"Did you really quit your job?"

"I really did. High time, too."

His mom sighed heavily. "I've never liked how your father forced you into the business before you ever had a chance to make a choice for yourself, but I'm also worried about you quitting without making a plan."

"What do you mean? I have a plan," he argued. "It's to move in with you and then make a new plan from there."

Brandon listened to the dead air as his mom once again struggled to find the right words. "Oh, honey. You know I love you, but we can't do that."

"Why not? Do you have some new boyfriend I don't know about?" He forced a laugh, not sure what answer he preferred.

"No, nothing like that. It's just..." She sucked in

another deep, shaky breath. "Well, you're more than old enough to lead your own life. Don't you think?"

Was his mother really shutting him out in his hour of need? She'd never done that before, and he sensed she didn't want to do it now. Surely if he reframed the problem, she'd come around.

"Yes, of course," he said. "But I also need time to regroup. I just quit on Dad less than an hour ago, and—"

"You quit without having a backup plan." She didn't sound angry, just very, very tired. "Most people can't get away with that. Welcome to the real world, Brandon. I'm glad you're finally joining us, but I am not going to enable you to be a spoiled trust fund baby for the rest of your life."

"Mom, what are you saying?"

"Go out and find a job. Make your own life."

"But—"

"I know you can do it, and I can send some money to help out, but I will not let you crash here, because I know it won't be temporary. If you're truly out from under your father's thumb, then use this chance to make a real grown-up life for yourself."

Wow. That had really just happened. His mother's refusal to help him was even more shocking than his father's prejudice.

He didn't say anything as he considered his mother's words. Apparently, this was too long a pause, because soon she said, "I love you, honey, and I know you can do this" and ended their call.

Well, there was a cold, hard dose of reality.

If he wasn't good enough for Ruby before, then he surely wasn't now that he'd lost everything that made him anyone.

He could admit defeat, or he could find a new way...

He at least needed to try.

12

*L*orna didn't return Ruby's frantic call until the next morning, and even then she seemed to be in a hurry.

"Don't worry," she said during their brief call. "No press is bad press, and this press is actually very good for us. What better way to empower plus-sized women to show them they can land any guy they want as long as they're wearing the right clothes?"

Thinking of the scathing article and the hundreds of bullying commenters who'd piled on as a way to sell more clothes made Ruby feel dirty. Would everything she did from now on be viewed through this money-hungry lens? "What about Brandon, though?" she asked Lorna, realizing that she already missed him like crazy, even though hardly any time had passed at all.

Lorna seemed startled by this question. "What about him? He's had way worse PR than this, and he's always bounced back before. And besides, that article was right. Those teas do awful things to your digestion."

They said goodbye, leaving Ruby with a giant mountain of work she couldn't ignore, no matter how heartsick this latest fiasco made her.

Diamond rolled over onto her back and whined, staring up at Ruby with big, brown eyes.

"At least I'll always have you," Ruby told the dog, plopping down onto the carpet beside her and offering a much-coveted belly rub.

This seemed to satisfy Diamond, but it did nothing to help Ruby. Would life forever be work and nothing more? She'd always loved designing beautiful clothes but had already started to question the many unwanted accessories that came tacked on to this new success. What good was any of this if she could say all the right words at press conferences but still have every decision she made outside of the studio ripped apart for all to see?

Brandon had practically been born into this

world. Even though it was too late for him to escape, he at least knew how to deftly navigate it.

Ruby, on the other hand, could still break free. She could call this whole thing off. She could walk away from her chain of retail shops, cancel her partnership with Lorna, and go back to designing for private clients, one at a time. It wouldn't be a glamorous life, but it could still be happy—and, most importantly, it could still be her own.

The door buzzed, startling Ruby from her thoughts.

"Hello?" she asked cautiously.

"It's Shasta," came the answer.

Oh, right! Her new assistant was set to start today.

Wait... It was only Saturday, and Ruby had told Shasta to come by Monday morning. Had she misremembered that? Probably, given how harried her mind was that morning.

"C'mon up," Ruby called, buzzing her new assistant in.

Two short minutes later, Shasta appeared upstairs, and Ruby ushered her inside.

"I thought I said Monday morning, but with how busy I've been, it's totally possible I made a mistake," Ruby said with a laugh, happy that her apartment wasn't too out of order. Soon they'd both be working at the new studio Lorna had secured for her uptown, but until then, it would certainly help to have some human assistance when it came to fulfilling her outstanding orders.

Shasta bit her lip and cast her eyes toward the floor. "No, you didn't make any mistake. Well, except for maybe hiring the wrong person."

Tension bubbled in Ruby's gut. She didn't know if she could handle any more bad news today—or ever for that matter. "What do you mean?" she asked softly, though her voice sounded strained to her own ears.

"Don't get me wrong." Shasta raised her eyes to Ruby's and hurried to clarify. "I'm so grateful that you chose me, but it's just that I got a better offer, so I'm going to have to decline yours."

Ruby nodded but didn't say anything aloud. Even with everything imploding in her relationship with Brandon, at least she had the comfort that things were going perfectly with her work. Until now.

"I thought maybe it would be easier if I dropped by and told you in person. I'm sorry." Shasta reached in for a hug, and Ruby returned the embrace, still dumbfounded.

"Um, thanks for letting me know," she said, leading her almost-assistant back to the door. "Good luck, Shasta."

"You, too," the friendly young woman called as she waggled her fingers at Ruby. "And congrats on the hottie boyfriend!"

Shasta was out the door before Ruby had the chance to correct her.

Brandon had been the perfect boyfriend, and Shasta had seemed like the perfect assistant. Both were too perfect for Ruby, apparently.

"Well, this stinks," she muttered to her curious corgi, crossing the tiny apartment to grab her laptop and open up her email. The other resumes she'd received still sat starred in a special folder. Thank goodness her organizational skills could still salvage this awful day.

She reviewed each resume a second time, even those she'd immediately canned.

No one was as good as Shasta which, of course, was why she'd been yanked away so fast. Figured.

Even though she'd received eleven applications, only one of them came anywhere close to Shasta's. And it was someone she'd already interviewed and hadn't cared much for on a personal level. Well, maybe both women had been too nervous to make a good first impression. She was Ruby's very first interview, after all.

Shaking her head, she dialed the number listed at the top of the resume in enormous font. "Hello, Heather?" she asked when the young woman picked up. "Are you still interested in that assistant position?"

*B*randon found a hotel to hunker down in for the night, but despite his best efforts, sleep wouldn't come. He passed the long hours by thumbing through Ruby's Instagram feed, smiling as he took in each photo of her taking selfies with Diamond, modeling new creations, being happy and living the life she'd built for herself.

Why had he waited so long to finally decide to grow up?

His mom was absolutely right to deny him help.

Whether or not Brandon did a good job for his father's company was beside the point. Everything had been handed to him, and he'd taken it all, even though he didn't much care for what was being served.

When they'd first met, Ruby had asked more

than once why he liked her, but this whole time he should have been the one demanding an explanation from her. Why would a smart, talented, successful, gorgeous woman ever want to be with a loser man child like him?

He knew Ruby saw more him for more than his looks. He just wished he knew what it was that had earned him a second glance.

Other than his mother, Ruby was the first to see him as someone separate from the company he represented. All the other women he'd dated briefly in the past seemed to view him more as a free ticket into the top parties or the most widely circulated gossip rags. They'd much rather to have been seen with him than listen to anything he might have to say.

They'd used him.

And he'd used them right back.

He'd never asked any of the Ashleighs, Kims, or Veronicas what they hoped to achieve in life. He'd enjoyed every moment spent dancing, flirting, carousing...

Until suddenly he hadn't.

The next morning, he thought back to the party where he'd first met Ruby several weeks ago. From that very first moment Lorna had forced an introduction between them, he could tell that she was different. It wasn't just her gorgeous smile and inviting curves, but more that she seemed to be the only person there who wasn't throwing herself on every celebrity in sight like some kind of crazed groupie.

She'd occupied her own space—*commanded it*—and even when she was being shy with him, she never backed away or gone to hide.

All Brandon ever did was hide. He hid behind his attractive body, behind his dad's money, behind all of it. He even hid from himself. Because now that his parents refused to bail him out of his latest mess-up, he had absolutely no idea what he should do next.

He was finally free! He could do anything he wanted!

But he hadn't the slightest idea what that might be.

How pathetic.

Sure, one of the friends he'd made over the years might be willing to give him a place to crash, but what would good that do? All that would accomplish is to further delay the problem—the problem that he didn't know his own heart.

Well, except for the piece of it that would always belong to Ruby.

He flicked his screen away from Ruby's Instagram profile and visited his main feed. There, he found various promotional posts he'd paid reality TV stars to make for the expensive Body by Price detox tea:

It keeps me strong!

It gives my skin a beautiful glow!

It tastes like a little cup of heaven!

Lies, all of it. Brandon knew that tea was crap, yet he'd still promoted it without shame for years. Now every ounce of shame he should have felt earlier crashed into him all at once like a tidal wave.

He should have known better. Should have been better.

Brandon felt lighter as he unfollowed each of the accounts and continued to move down his feed. From the overly posed pictures to the flashy shows of wealth, it was all so unbelievably shallow.

Unfollow, unfollow, unfollow.

But then he spied a photo that made him pause. A lopsided smile crept up his face as he studied the bright screen before him.

Fresh air, fresh outlook, Ruby had captioned her newest post. The picture showed her feet laced up in bright red walking shoes with Diamond smiling up at the camera, wearing a matching red bandana around her fluffy little neck.

Brandon resisted the temptation to press the heart button, not wanting to give Ruby anything new to worry about. This showed another big difference between them. He'd begged his mommy for help and then decided to hide out and mope when she'd told him "no."

Ruby, on the other hand, was out there carrying on with her day, with her life. If she'd felt bad at all, she decided to make things better rather than to simply hope they'd get better on their own.

This. This was why he didn't deserve her.

Or rather, he didn't deserve her *yet,* but—God willing—he'd find a way to earn a second chance at the happily ever after he knew they could have once they made it through this unfortunate brush with the cruel Central Park paparazzi.

There would be other challenges. All other relationships had them, too. But he could fix things, first for himself, and then for the two of them together.

He wasn't ready to give up on his dream girl yet.

And he was pretty sure he had the perfect idea of how he could get her back.

13

*R*uby welcomed her new assistant, Heather, into her apartment-slash-workspace two days later. This time the girl arrived ten minutes late, but she did apologize for the tardiness, which was at least a step in the right direction.

"It takes forever to get a cab around here," she moaned, handing Ruby one of the two Starbucks cups she held in her hands. Another good move on Heather's part.

"Thank you for this!" Ruby said as she raised her cup in salute.

A smile flashed across Heather's pretty face. "No problem. I wasn't sure what you liked, so I got you the same thing as me—a half-caf latte with soy, no sweetener."

Ruby preferred full-caf caramel macchiatos but was too grateful for the unexpected gesture of kindness to say anything other than a sincere thank you. Her usual or not, the drink did offer a much-needed pick-me-up and gave them both a nice, casual way to start their first day together.

Heather took a seat on Ruby's couch and crossed her legs at the knee. "So, where do we start?" she asked, tapping her nicely manicured fingers on her knee as she glanced around the small apartment. "Oh, we never did discuss my pay, by the way."

Oh, shoot. That would have been an important thing to discuss *before* officially hiring her. "Right, sorry about that," Ruby sputtered. "How does twenty per hour sound?"

The other woman made a face, which quickly dissolved into a tight-lipped smile. "Too low. Make it thirty and you've got yourself a deal."

"Yeah, sure," Ruby said, trying not to let sticker shock set in. She knew that even the twenty dollars per hour she'd initially offered was a very fair rate, but maybe Heather would surprise her and easily earn those increased wages.

"Perfect. Thank you." Heather smiled again and brushed off her lap, which Diamond took as an invite to join her up on the couch. The little tan and white dog clambered onto her jean-clad lap and gave her an enthusiastic kiss on the arm.

Heather's smile dissolved in an instant and she bolted to her feet. "I forgot about the dog," she said as panic mounted in her expression. "Do you have a lint roller somewhere around here?"

"C'mere, Di," Ruby called, then hoisted the dog into her arms and gave her a peck between the ears. "As long as we're not meeting with clients you don't need to worry about a little extra corgi glitter."

Heather continued to frantically brush off her lap, which only spread the dog hair around more. "Corgi glitter?"

Ruby laughed at the disgusted expression that crossed Heather's face. "Yeah, it's what we call their hair because it gets everywhere. I even have a shirt that says *this isn't dog hair on my shirt, it's corgi glitter*. I mean, in case you want to change into something more comfortable."

"That's okay. I don't think it would fit."

Ruby studied the girl's waifish build, which she'd dressed in skinny jeans and an oddly cut structured blouse that she could have only made herself. Stiletto heels completed the look and also explained why she'd needed a cab for such a short distance.

"Well," she said at last, clapping her hands

together after setting Diamond back on the floor. "Let's get you started. Can you start by taking inventory? Just a general reporting of what we have in stock along with how much."

"Inventory?" Heather looked even more disgusted than she had before. "I thought I'd be designing—or at least sewing—clothes. Your job description said—"

Ruby was quick to cut her off. "That I need a fashion assistant, yes. You can work your way up to the more glamorous tasks, but right now I really need help with the inventory, please."

Heather nodded and headed in the direction Ruby pointed so that she could begin the unwanted task. Diamond followed happily, taking a playful nip at Heather's heels. Well, at least she knew not to complain any more than she already had.

Ruby felt less and less certain things would work out but still hoped Heather would prove her wrong. She was mentally preparing a task list for the rest of the day when her phone rang with a call from Lorna's assistant.

"Hey, Marian. What's up?" Ruby said by way of greeting, heading out in the hall to gain a small measure of privacy.

"Lorna wanted me to give you a heads up about

another string of press interviews and networking events she has scheduled for you this coming week. Okay if I email over the details?" Marian's voice was as bright and chipper as always. Sometimes Ruby wondered if she might have a hidden line pumping espresso straight into her veins.

"Yeah, sure. Thank you," Ruby said, feeling tired when comparing herself to the other woman's unending energy. But if Marian noticed Ruby's lack of pep, she certainly didn't let on.

They exchanged a few quick pleasantries before saying goodbye, and when Ruby returned to the apartment, Heather glanced over at her briefly, then threw herself back into her task. They didn't know each other well enough to share things like this. Soon she hoped that would change.

Ruby also longed to call Brandon for a pep talk, but she'd just have to keep his previous advice close to her heart. From now on she'd have to handle things herself and hope that eventually things would get easier.

*B*randon checked his reflection in the shiny gold elevator doors and forced a smile. "I can do this," he murmured under his breath before pushing the call button. "I can."

He rocked back and forth on the balls of his feet before finally taking a deep breath and striding into the waiting elevator. This impossibly tall skyscraper had more floors than he'd had girlfriends, and today he'd be going all the way to the top.

He was surprised how easy it had been landing a meeting with Lorna Stevens. Most big business people had too many obligations and too little time —and that included his father. But Lorna had accepted his request and scheduled their meeting with only a couple days' notice on his part.

That had hardly given him enough time to lay out his plan, but he also appreciated the rush of this unintentionally tight deadline. The sooner he could fix his life, the sooner he could get his Ruby back.

With one last internal affirmation, he stepped off the elevator and onto the top floor. The entire level was walled in with floor to ceiling windows, which immediately made Brandon feel a bit seasick. He'd never been afraid of heights before, but he'd also never been more than one-hundred stories high with just a thin sheet of glass standing between him and certain death.

"Mr. Price?" an attractive middle-aged woman called to him from behind the enormous modular desk that sat in the rear center of the room. She wore a controlled smile with a lavender blouse and her hair was swept back in a tight updo.

He nodded and approached with a hand extended in greeting. "Good morning."

She stood and returned the handshake. "I'm Ms. Stevens's assistant Marian. You'll actually be meeting with me today," she informed him, stepping to the side as she came out from behind the giant desk. "Are you ready?"

Brandon nodded, then followed her down a hidden side hallway. He was almost certain he'd scheduled his meeting with the big boss, not her assistant. Would Marian understand his request and be willing to help? Brandon wasn't so sure.

He waited politely now as she asked another employee to cover the front desk for a little while. "I thought I had a meeting scheduled with Lorna," he said, hoping he didn't sound rude or ungrateful. "She told me to be here at ten o'clock."

"Yes, you're meeting with Lorna *through* me. Tell me everything you wanted to say to her, and I'll give

her the condensed version during our daily staff
meeting." She turned in the narrow hallway so that
they stood face-to-face. The abruptness of the move
startled him and he quickly forgot his whispered
pep talk from the elevator quickly forgotten.

"That is okay, isn't it?" she asked with a slight
frown.

Well, obviously it had to be okay. Brandon
couldn't see a way to make his plan work without the
billionairess's help, and clearly he needed to go
through Marian to get to her. "Yeah, sure. Just caught
me off-guard is all."

Marian motioned toward the giant conference
table and waited for Brandon to take a seat. He
chose a neon yellow leather chair with a low back
and sat heavily, while his interviewer chose a simple
white chair at the head of the table.

She folded her hands on the table in front of her
and narrowed his eyes at him. "Now tell me. How
can we help you today, Mr. Price?"

Brandon's mouth suddenly felt very dry. Should
he wait to see if Marian would offer him a drink, ask
for one himself, or just get on with it? He cleared his
throat and wiped his sweaty palms on his trousers.

"You look nervous," Marian said with an understanding smile. "Don't be. Lorna's always been

generous with her time and money and you're an old family friend, so as long as you have a reasonably decent proposal, I'm sure she'd be happy to invest."

"No," Brandon corrected with an emphatic shake of his head. "I'm not asking for any money."

Marian raised an eyebrow, uncrossed, and re-crossed her legs. "Oh? Well, now I'm really interested in what you have to say."

"No money," Brandon repeated. "Just a little bit of press."

"For a new venture of yours?" She spun her chair slightly to one side and then the other. It seemed like Marian never stopped moving. Probably never stopped thinking, either.

"Not exactly." He took another deep breath. At least she seemed genuinely interested in what he had to say. Everything could still happen exactly as he planned. He just needed to speak his needs clearly and hope that Marian would adequately express his passion when presenting these meeting notes on to her boss.

"I've got it all planned out," he said with what he hoped was an ingratiating smile. "First I need a press conference and then…"

14

*T*he next two weeks passed quickly for Ruby. Between the dizzying blur of work, media interviews, and training her new assistant, she regrettably found almost no time to rest and recharge. Thankfully, Heather did rise to every challenge Ruby gave her, earning both her employer's trust and the inflated salary she'd demanded. Heather had also formed a tentative friendship with Diamond and often walked the dog around town on her lunch break.

Yes, Ruby felt relieved knowing that Heather was there to keep the corgi company while she rushed off to yet another press conference that afternoon. It was also nice that their work wouldn't come to a full stop in her absence. She'd taken a bit of a gamble and, thank goodness, it had paid off—at least as far as Heather was concerned.

She still missed talking with Brandon throughout the day, but at least their romance hadn't gotten the chance to go very far before it came to an abrupt end. Their friendship, on the other hand? That was harder to let go.

Ruby had successfully navigated a couple press conferences without him now, and everything had seemed to go just fine.

Maybe she really didn't need him anymore.

Or maybe she was just making excuses.

Whatever the case, she had this one last conference and then she was free for another few weeks before Lorna sent her on another junket. Ruby knew Lorna was the expert, but all this talking seemed silly. She'd much rather be *showing* the world what she was made of by presenting beautiful new fashions rather than simply promising everyone that they'd soon be coming.

This was especially true, considering everyone tended to ask the same questions over and over... and over again. Well, except when they chose to boldly inquire about the paparazzi photos of her and Brandon taken together in Central Park.

"No comment at this time," had been her response each of the times her brief relationship with Brandon was questioned. Hopefully enough time had passed that everyone at today's press interview would have moved on from her personal life.

She tucked her hair behind her ears and tiptoed toward the podium, more than ready to get this over with so she could go back to finishing the sketches for the working woman line for her fall collection. The room before her was completely empty, however—not a reporter or even a member of Lorna's staff in sight.

Had she gotten the time wrong? Or maybe the address? Perhaps the world just didn't care about Ruby Ross anymore, and if that was the case, Lorna would not be happy with her. *Crud.*

Just as she was about to search for someone she could ask about her startling lack of an audience, a door at the rear of the room opened outward and admitted a single suited figure.

Brandon.

"What are you doing here?" she asked, part of her wanting to run to him and the other part too frightened to move.

"I'll ask the questions, if you don't mind," he said,

holding up a small Steno notepad and gracing her with his signature lopsided grin.

"Now's not a good time," she argued as she placed her hands on each side of the podium and pressed down hard in a meager attempt to brace herself for whatever came next. "I have a press conference. At least, I think I do."

His smile widened and he sunk into one of the chairs that sat close to the front of the room. "Yeah, I'm the one who called it. Nobody else is coming."

"What? Why would you do that?"

"To talk to you. On the record." He waved his thick notepad again.

Ruby swallowed hard. It felt so good to see him again even if this whole situation had yet to make any sense. "Okay, go ahead," she said, her voice shaking but her body remaining strong and poised.

"Excellent." Brandon grabbed the pen he'd kept stashed behind his ear and let it hover over the paper. "How has it been working with Lorna Stevens on the development of your new retail chain?"

She rattled off her usual answer, the same one Brandon had coached her on several weeks ago.

He nodded and scribbled something on his pad. "And it's my understanding that a few weeks back you had a run in with the paparazzi. What was that like?"

Normally, she'd answer this line of questioning with "no comment." But this was Brandon. She had to give him a better answer than that.

"It was uncomfortable," she said, thinking back to that wretched day, the day that had spoiled everything between them. "Mostly because they said very cruel things about my friend."

He kept his face expressionless as he asked, "That friend. Would it happen to be Brandon Price?"

"It would." She chanced a small, sad smile, but Brandon charged ahead to his next question without lingering.

"Uh huh. And what's he been up to lately?"

Ruby suddenly felt very uncomfortable, standing there and waiting to see where Brandon was going with this. She hated the way things had unraveled between them, but she also didn't quite know how to fix it—or even if it *should* be fixed. "I don't know," she mumbled. "We've sort of fallen out of touch."

"Why?" He lifted his eyes to meet her, and they just stared at each other across that large, empty room.

Finally, Ruby licked her lips and said, "I'm not

sure I know the answer to that either. Maybe to protect him."

"Protect him? They said some pretty awful things about you, too."

She nodded. "As much as it hurts, I'm used to being called the fat girl. What I'm not used to is having my friends' ethics questioned on the sole basis of hanging out with me."

Brandon set the notepad and pen down onto the chair beside him. "Do you miss him?" he asked, regarding her with a broken expression. Finally she could see how much he was hurting, too.

Ruby sucked in a deep breath and tried not to blush beneath his hot gaze. "Every single day," she murmured.

*B*randon had prepared himself well for this moment, going over each question in his mind along with the possible answers Ruby might give. He hadn't readied himself, however, for how hard it would be to keep his distance the moment they locked eyes from across the room.

That was part of the reason he how decided to veer away from the plan. When Ruby admitted that she missed him every single day, he stood and asked, "You keep referring to him as your friend. Is that all he is to you?"

"We tried to keep it that way, but then there were these two amazing kisses, and..." She stopped speaking and looked away.

Brandon's breath hitched in his throat. Even his heartbeat slowed as he waited to hear whichever words she planned to say next. "And?" he urged.

"Well, I'd never been kissed that way before," she said, raising her eyes back to his slowly.

And just like that, Brandon couldn't keep his distance anymore. Without any further question, he sped over to Ruby and placed his hand gently on top of hers. "In what way?" he murmured.

Ruby hesitated for only a second before throwing her arms around his neck and bringing her face close. "I don't actually know that I can describe it."

He inched closer until his lips brushed the soft skin just to the side of her mouth. "Then show me," he whispered, staying close.

She raised her fingers to his cheek and pushed his mouth onto hers, and for one glorious moment, all was right with the world again.

But then she pulled back too soon and looked up

at Brandon with watery eyes. "Like that," she said with a sad smile.

Brandon brushed a lock of hair behind Ruby's ear and caressed her cheek with the backs of his folded fingers. "Did you really send me away because you were worried about *my* reputation?" He'd always assumed that she was the one who'd been hurting, not that she'd secretly been worrying about him this whole time.

"Yes," she admitted with a sad sigh.

He hugged her tight, hoping it would help to take some of their shared pain away. "The only thing that hurt me was how much I missed you."

"I'm sorry," she whispered into his shirt.

"Don't be. Maybe everything's happened exactly as it was meant to."

If someone had asked Brandon earlier whether he believed in fate, he would have laughed them right out of the room. Now it really did feel as if some divine force—maybe God—had always planned for him to meet Ruby, to lose her, and then to work hard to improve himself as part of his desperation to get her back.

She raised her head and searched his eyes. "Can we try again?" Ruby whispered, then bit her lip, waiting for his answer.

"Yes, that's what I want more than anything. But—"

"But?" Her eyes darted from side to side as she studied him, a look of confusion pinching her features.

"Not yet," he said, even though it pained him to speak these two little words.

Ruby pressed her lips in a thin line. "Then when?"

"When I've earned the right to date you by becoming a better man."

"I don't understand."

"You will." He kissed her on the cheek. "Soon, I hope."

She frowned, and he hated knowing that was his fault. He'd wanted to keep it all a secret, but now knew he had to at least explain himself a little bit.

"Ruby," he said, taking both of her hands in his. "I've never had to work hard for anything in my life. Not once. My job, money, looks, all of it was handed to me without having to do anything on my part. I've never had to question what tomorrow would bring or take a gamble on a big idea. My future has always been secure, but it's never belonged to me. Not really."

"What are you saying?"

Brandon could tell she wanted to support his needs but was having a hard time understanding them in that moment. She didn't know what it was like to be embarrassed of the person you'd become, to desperately need to make a change and make it now.

"I've never had to work hard for anything in my life," he repeated, stroking her hair softly as he spoke. "But I want you to be the first. Can you give me some time to sort some things out?"

"Don't you want to be with me?" Tears threatened to spill from her large eyes, which now appeared bluer than ever.

"More than anything," he promised, hoping that she would finally believe him, that she would understand why things needed to happen this way. "But you deserve the best version of myself I can possibly be and I'm working really hard to make that happen."

She nodded, then leaned her head on Brandon's shoulder. "I'll wait for you then. As long as you need."

"I'm not asking you to put your life on hold—only that when I'm ready you'll consider giving me a second chance to make things right."

They kissed again, short and mournful, both knowing it was a way of saying goodbye.

Brandon pulled away first.

"I'll be thinking only of you," he promised anew. "And I'll come back to you just as soon as I can."

15

*A*nother three weeks flew by. Everything was happening so quickly in preparation for Ruby's new retail chain, and while she was beyond excited, she'd also become quite exhausted.

Today was a big day because she, Diamond, and Heather were moving into their new studio space. Lorna had also hired more than a dozen consultants to help with everything from brand positioning to the interior blueprint for her forthcoming stores. Her new office had a large open area with several workstations sprinkled throughout the room and a row of private offices lined along two walls forming a big L.

It was far larger than the previous workspace Ruby kept in her tiny apartment, and she had a hard time believing it was all hers. Well, at least for now. Soon she and Lorna would begin hiring the members of what would become her core team.

And she thought the publicity stuff was hard!

Now people were bandying around terms like ROI and KPI and other acronyms she'd needed to have translated just to follow the conversation. Ruby just wanted to design clothes that made women feel beautiful and powerful. All these other parts that came with her new success made her head spin, but she was also committed to learning everything in time—something she didn't seem to have in abundance lately.

The few moments she found herself alone and without a task to keep herself busy, she thought of Brandon. He'd disappeared almost completely from the public eye this past month, and that worried her. She knew he was probably fine, but she couldn't help but wonder where he was and what he was doing. Would he be back soon as he'd promised?

She allowed herself to check his social media platforms and Google once per day for any kind of updates, but each time came up short. Whatever Brandon was doing, he'd somehow managed to keep it private from anyone who was watching—and, unfortunately, that included her.

The few friends she kept up with had all inquired about what had happened to Brandon and whether they were still an item. Luckily, it was easy to brush their questions aside, given that these exchanges only happened online or over text. Ruby didn't have the time to meet up in person. She didn't have the time to do anything but work, and she was okay with that.

It helped keep her focused, kept her from missing Brandon and wondering whether he'd ever come back to her as he'd promised.

Diamond nudged Ruby's bare shin with her cold, wet nose, then barked when Ruby glanced down at her.

"I know you're still here for me, Di," she said, picking up the heavy ball of fur and cuddling the corgi to her chest.

Diamond gave Ruby a series of licks on her cheek, then rewarded her with a cute doggie smile.

"You're right," Ruby said. "It's not time to worry. It's time to be happy. Right?"

Diamond barked again. Whether this was because Ruby had trained the dog that when she raised her voice in a question some kind of response was needed, or because Diamond barked at almost everything, anyway, Ruby couldn't be too sure.

She did feel comforted, though.

Diamonds really were a girl's best friend.

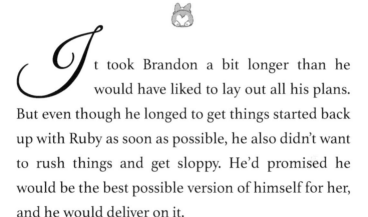

*I*t took Brandon a bit longer than he would have liked to lay out all his plans. But even though he longed to get things started back up with Ruby as soon as possible, he also didn't want to rush things and get sloppy. He'd promised he would be the best possible version of himself for her, and he would deliver on it.

Brandon had already filed for a business license with the state, submitted trademarks for his new company name and logo, and written up his formal governing articles. He even had a new website built and ready to deploy just as soon as he took care of one last important piece of business.

Deep breaths, deep breaths, he reminded himself while he waited inside yet another conference room. Before he'd done most of his work at conventions, in fitness centers, or restaurants. He wondered if the sudden abundance of in-office meetings meant he was, indeed, moving up in the world.

Today's conference room belonged to the Body by Price headquarters. He'd gone through the official channels to book an important meeting with his father but had asked that the purpose of the meeting not be revealed until he arrived in person to explain. Brandon needed his father to consider his proposal without letting it get shaded by their recent past.

Would this one crucial meeting be enough to show his father how much he had changed? He realized he was asking for this one hour to overwrite their years of tension, but things hadn't always been this way between them. Hopefully it wasn't too late to go back, to start over.

"Here to ask for your job back?" his dad said with a smirk as he entered the room and settled into his favorite chair. "It's about time. We have a lot of catching up to do."

"No," Brandon said, standing firm in front of the projector. "I'm here to present a new proposal." He pressed a button on his laptop and brought up the title slide of his presentation.

"'The new Body by Price, a plan to strengthen the brand and meet core customer needs'," his father read aloud. "What's this?"

"It's exactly what it says." Brandon stepped to the side so that the screen was in full view. "My plan for suggested improvements for Body at Price."

His father continued to study the words

projected in front of him rather than looking at his son. "What do you want, Brandon?"

"For you to listen and, if you like my plan, implement it. I'm not asking for capital or connections or any of that. But I do want you to be among the first to see what my new business can do firsthand."

"A new business?" Finally, his father turned his attention toward him. This was it. Time to show what he was made of.

Brandon clicked through to the next slide. If his dad planned to question everything he said, this would take forever. He was going to go ahead and deliver his plan confidently because he knew it was good, and he hoped as they got further along his father would see that, too.

Brandon started with some choice compliments that he knew would make his father more receptive to the later criticism. "Body by Price is the biggest and most respected health and fitness brand in the country, but that doesn't mean it can't be even better."

Click.

A photo of Brandon posing and posturing with his muscular arms raised overhead filled the screen. "To start, the current spokesmodel isn't relatable to the core consumer demographic. Since more than eighty-five percent of customers are women trying to lose weight, a more relatable choice might be…"

Click. Click. Click.

He took his father through a series of pictures showing him the new type of model he had in mind. "These women are smart, confident, beautiful, and successful. They've gained a few pounds while conquering the business world and growing their families, but now they're ready to get back on track."

He risked a quick glance toward his father and found that he was nodding along with each point Brandon made. "They're relatable, attainable, and people will root for them. Body by Price is a real brand for real people. These women are actual participants in one of our fitness classes and swear by Body by Price."

Next, he took his father through each testimonial he gathered. "As you can see, they are the best spokesmodels—our real customers. Happy customers."

Brandon's father steepled his fingers in front of him and nodded. He didn't praise his son's idea, but he also didn't turn it down. "What else have you got?" he asked.

"I have nineteen more suggestions—some big, some small, but all aimed at helping boost public perception of Body by Price and thus also boosting revenue."

"You really did all this without expecting anything in return?"

Brandon shook his head. "No, there is something I want."

His father exhaled slowly and motioned for Brandon to go ahead with his request.

Brandon moved in front of the screen and stood right before his father. "I want you to go back to being my dad, to support me in my new business, and understand that this is what I want to do with my life now."

"Is that all?"

"That's all."

"Well, go ahead. I want to hear your other nineteen points."

Brandon had to avoid giving a little cheer when he realized that he had finally landed his father's blessing for the first time in many, many years. No more impossible rules, no more strained relationship. He was well on his way to having a job he loved, a dad who loved him, and a girl who...

Well, that was yet to be determined.

First he'd focus on finishing this presentation

strong. Then he could carry on with the next stage of his plan.

He clicked to a new slide and smiled proudly as he presented his next point. "Point two, we need to discuss retiring the detox tea..."

16

*R*uby bit down hard on her lip, but still the tears she'd hope to keep at bay came spilling out.

"I love it," she cried breathlessly, raising both her hands to cover her mouth. "It's perfect."

Heather placed an arm around her boss's shoulders and leaned in close to study the newly approved logo for Ruby's retail chain. "It's so you," she agreed.

They both stared for a little while longer, admiring how the letter R stood in a bold black serif font—classic just like Ruby's fashions. Next to it was the image of an impressive red gemstone shaded to give it a 3D effect, and that was then followed by two big black S's. In front of the big *R* in Ross her first name RUBY was spelled out in black sans serif letters written sideways and running from the bottom of the line to the top.

RUBY R●SS

"Classic with a bit of pizazz," Ruby mumbled, still unable to pull her eyes away.

"Your favorite colors, too," Heather pointed out, alluding to the fact that most of Ruby's clothes were designed in black, white, and red.

"I don't know if I'll ever be able to stop staring at it," Ruby confessed. "It's like suddenly all of this became very, very real."

Heather chuckled. "The money, press conferences, parties, and new studio didn't do that for you?" She shook her head and crossed the room back to her own desk. "When I get to where you are, I'll be celebrating every single moment."

That was the thing about Heather—she never hid her ambition. At first that bothered Ruby, but now she appreciated how hard her assistant was willing to work on her behalf. Because, as she'd said many times, she was "filing it all away for later."

Some more time passed. Ruby had no idea how much.

But eventually one of Heather's skinny wrists darted in front of Ruby and a moment later she nudged her boss's laptop closed.

"Hey," Ruby whined. "I was looking at that."

Heather pushed back the other woman's wheeled desk chair and placed her thin body directly in front of her. "Not anymore you're not. It's already late in the day anyway. Let's go celebrate! C'mon!" She grabbed Ruby's hand and pulled her to her feet.

"Jeez. What is with everyone always forcing me to celebrate?"

"Everyone?" Heather asked curiously.

Oops. She hadn't meant to talk about Brandon. It had just slipped out. "Well, you and Brandon, at least," she mumbled dismissively.

Heather crossed her arms and narrowed her eyes. "I thought you two broke up."

"We did, I guess."

"You want him back," Heather said, her eyes aglow with mischief. "I don't blame you. He's one of the hottest guys I've ever seen. If it were me, I would have found anyway to make things work."

Ruby shrugged, more than ready to change the subject. "It's not that simple."

"Yeah, but it doesn't need to be that hard, either."

"If I agree to head out early to celebrate, do you promise to stop talking about Brandon?"

Heather let out a sigh. "Yeah. Sure. Whatever," was all she said before pulling Ruby out of the studio.

They stopped by Ruby's apartment for a quick change of clothes—Heather insisted she wear her red leather pants and an asymmetrical black tank—then headed to one of the clubs near Heather's campus.

"I think I'm too old for this place," Ruby pointed out.

"Yeah, but I'm too young for any of the bars, so..." She gave her boss a winning smile. "Compromise."

That was what happened when your assistant was only twenty years old, Ruby supposed. At least she'd have a legitimately good excuse to bow out early, especially if Heather found a gentleman suitor, which Ruby had no doubt would happen given how gorgeous her young, blonde assistant was.

It surprised her, though, when a tall man in glasses set his sights on her of all people. "Are you a professor, too?" he asked by way of opening. "Or maybe a grad student?"

"Neither," Ruby answered, taking another sip of her Diet Coke. "Just here with a friend to celebrate."

"Mind if I join you?" he asked glibly.

Ruby took a moment to study him. He was definitely good looking, and normally she'd be flattered by his attention. But she still saw Brandon's face whenever she closed her eyes, still wanted to believe he'd come back to her soon. This was especially true since accidentally talking about him with Heather earlier that evening.

"Um, are you hitting on me?" she said with a polite smile. Definitely not smooth, but then again, she didn't need to impress anyone.

"And here I worried it wasn't obvious," he said, sliding into the seat beside her.

"You seem really nice, but I have a boyfriend," she told him with an apologetic smile. It was easier than trying to explain what she and Brandon were to each other or how their relationship was currently on hold.

"Oh, I see. Sorry to have bothered you." He slipped off the seat just as seamlessly as he'd slipped on, then nodded to her before turning away in search of someone else to occupy his attention.

"Have a good evening!" Ruby called after him with a wave, feeling like the most inept person in all of New York City.

"Ruby!" Heather growled, running over to her with a fresh Diet Coke in her hands. "That guy was hot. Did you get his number?"

Ruby swallowed hard and shook her head.

"All right, that's it," Heather moaned. "I officially don't know what to do with you anymore."

"Then it's a good thing I'm in charge," Ruby said with a laugh.

After that brief hiccough, she did enjoy her evening...

But she also couldn't stop thinking about how much better it would be if Brandon were at her side.

*B*randon shrugged into the jacket of the new suit he'd bought just for this day. It was made of a fine black silk, and he'd paired it with a red collared shirt and white tie that sported a subtle paisley pattern in ivory. He looked sharp and had worked hard to get to this moment. After all, it could change his entire life.

And things were already off to a great start.

His father had been so impressed with his full audit proposal for Body by Price that he'd insisted on paying Brandon for all his hard work, refusing to accept no for an answer. As a compromise, they'd agreed that Brandon would move into their New York apartment until he found a place all his own.

That's where he was now as he prepared to put the final step of his big plan in action. He'd even hired his former stylist, Florence, to help make sure he looked his absolute best.

And he was ready for whatever came next, because he knew he'd given it everything he had. He'd committed to a plan, followed through and—no matter what—his life had already changed in a huge way.

Florence hesitated after finishing with Brandon's old-fashioned shave. She brought a hand to her chin as she studied him wordlessly.

"What is it?" he asked, doubts now forming along the edges of his mind.

She shifted her weight from one foot to the other and hummed a few beats before finally saying, "It's just, you look so tired, and I really do think you'd benefit from—"

"A touch of eyeliner maybe?" he asked with a smirk.

Florence nodded, but still looked unsure. "We don't have to, but..." Her words trailed off, and Brandon picked them up with a laugh.

"Go ahead, but make sure it's subtle. I can use all the help I can get today, even if that means going a little bit outside of my comfort zone." He closed his eyes and leaned back with a heavy exhale.

"Why so nervous?" Florence asked, leaning in close to rub a sweet-smelling lotion into his face.

"It's only the most important meeting of my life," Brandon said, fidgeting with his hands in his lap as he opened his eyes again. "Any advice for me?"

"Yeah," Florence said with a far-away smile. "Be yourself."

He let out a sarcastic laugh. This was just like the time Ruby had asked his advice prior to her press conference and he'd given her the most cliched answer possible.

"I mean it," the stylist insisted, wagging her finger at him as she set the lotion aside and reached into her gigantic box of cosmetics.

Brandon thought about this for a moment as he closed his eyes so that she could apply the liner Florence seemed to swear by. "The thing is," he said slowly, trying to remain still. "I think I am. You know, really being myself. And it's for the first time in my entire life." He raised his lashes and found Florence hovering close while wearing a broad smile.

"Take a look," Florence said, holding up a hand mirror before him.

"Hey, I really do look more awake," Brandon said, unsure of why this surprised him. His trusted stylist had never steered him wrong before. They'd only stopped working together because he'd stopped working for his father's company.

"Told you." She patted him on the shoulder, then gave it a quick squeeze. "Good luck out there today."

And that was his cue.

It was time to initiate the final step of his plan.

Brandon was more than ready for whatever came next.

17

*R*uby paused to admire her new logo, which had been expertly painted onto the wall that flanked the posh seating area directly opposite the main entrance to her studio.

This new addition gave the already comfortable space even more personality. It also made it feel as if the space truly belonged to her. It did have her name on it, after all.

Heather had taken the day off in order to work on an important school project, which left Ruby and Diamond alone in the big, empty office. She and Lorna's assistant, Marian, had finished interviewing job candidates for the various corporate positions, and now they were waiting on Lorna's board to make the final picks. That meant that soon the cavernous studio would be bustling with activity, and Ruby couldn't wait for the full team to be here and working together.

For now, she returned to her email, amazed at how many of the hours in her day were already taken up by this particular task.

Sensing the boredom ahead, Diamond went to snooze in her fancy new doggie bed that had been an office-warming gift from Ruby's parents.

She'd spent at least an hour tending to the somewhat mindless task of cleaning out her inbox, when suddenly the little dog began barking up a storm.

"Di, stop that!" Ruby scolded, rubbing her temples with firm circles. "Come here."

The corgi ran quickly across the polished wood floors, but didn't stop at her owner's workstation as commanded. Instead, she went straight for the door and began to scratch at the tiny crack beneath it while continuing to bark, whine, and whimper all at full volume.

"Diamond, enough of that!" Ruby said, getting up from her desk and marching toward the door to retrieve the little terror. She'd just bent over to collect the thirty-pound bundle of fluff when the door swung open and knocked her back onto the hard floor with Diamond landing on her lap. *Oof!*

A pair of nicely polished shoes attached to sleek black trousers rushed toward her, a deep voice muttering apologies.

She craned her neck upward and locked eyes with the man just as he was helping to pull her back to her feet. "Brandon!" she cried, throwing her arms around him in a tight embrace. "It's you!"

"It's me," he confirmed with a bashful smile. "What a way to make an entrance, huh?"

But Ruby felt too overjoyed to be embarrassed. "You came back," she said as she squeezed him even tighter. "You finally came back to me."

"It's so good to see you, too, Ruby." He slowly extricated himself from her hug, but his smile didn't waver for even a second. "I'll have you know I'm not here on a social visit, though. I'm here for a job interview."

"A job interview? But…"

"Just hear me out?" he requested, his adorable dimple making an appearance now as his smile grew even larger.

She nodded and led him deeper into the studio where a posh red couch and two black and white striped club chairs formed a seating area.

Brandon let out a low whistle. "Nice setup you have here. I love the logo."

"Thanks," she muttered as she tucked a stray piece of hair behind her ear and tried to remember what she was wearing today. As it turned out, she'd dressed in one of her comfier ensembles. The loose-fitting garment weren't what she'd have chosen to wear during their reunion, but at least she was presentable.

Still, Brandon's sudden appearance seemed to have addled her brain, but at least she had a lot of very recent interviewing experience and knew she could get through this. And then when they were done, perhaps he'd be ready to talk about their future as a couple, too.

"Now..." She folded her hands in her lap and crossed her legs at the ankles. "What position were you interested in?"

"Image consultant," Brandon said confidently, passing her a small file folder. "Inside you'll find my resume, mission statement, and a list of services I offer my clients."

"Your clients?" she asked as she rifled through the papers inside.

His voice remained strong, confident. "Well, my hypothetical clients. I'm hoping you'll be my first *official* client."

"Yours? Does that mean...?"

"That I handed in my resignation at Body by Price and have put in all the legwork to start my own company? Yes, that's exactly what I did."

She closed the folder in her lap and leaned closer. He'd laid out all the information very carefully, but she'd much rather talk with him now that he was here. "What's your new company called?"

Brandon swallowed hard, appearing nervous for the first time since he's arrived. "Diamond Media Coaching or DMC for short. I hope that's okay. I didn't want to use the Price name, and, well—"

She laughed as the corgi came running over in response to hearing her name.

"That's more than okay," Ruby said. "As you can see, she's flattered."

He pulled a large dog bone out of the briefcase he'd brought with him and offered the treat to Diamond, who eagerly accepted.

"So, what can DMC do for me?" Ruby asked, returning to the interview even though she was dying to ask him at least a hundred other, more personal questions.

"The question is what can't we do," he said with a wink, then broke out into a boisterous laugh. "Just kidding. That's a horrible line, and with our help, you can avoid accidentally slipping into clichés when meeting with the media and instead use your words, your look, your presence to command the respect you deserve."

"I like that," she said with a nod. "What else have you got?"

Brandon licked his lips, then offered her a genuinely huge smile. "I'll tell you once you *tell me* whether I'm hired."

*B*randon waited anxiously for Ruby's verdict, but instead of offering him the job, she just laughed and laughed, unable to take her eyes off him.

"Brandon, I was never not going to hire you," she admitted a few moments later.

He wanted to know he had earned her respect, that she liked what she'd inspired in him. "Even so. You're the one who inspired me in this new venture, and I want to make sure I'm doing you proud," he explained.

"You've laid everything out really well, and the help you gave me already has been priceless. Of course, I'm proud of you." She uncrossed and recrossed her legs, setting his portfolio to the side.

"Are you proud of yourself?"

It was a good question—one he knew she'd ask —and he was ready for it. "For once, I actually am. I kind of feel like my whole life has been leading to this point. Does that sound completely ridiculous or what?"

"It doesn't sound ridiculous at all," Ruby said, dropping her voice to a husky whisper as she studied him with shining, blue eyes.

"So, you'll hire me?" he asked, then held his breath as he waited for her response.

Her smile comforted him, assured him that nothing between the two of them had changed despite all their time apart. "Um, I'm pretty sure I already did," she said, her smile widening.

"Okay, I'm still hired then?" he asked with a laugh.

"Congrats, Brandon Price." Ruby stood and extended a hand toward him. "You're still hired."

"Thank you. Although there is still the small matter of my pay?" He used his hold on her hand to pull her in close, his gaze intense.

She widened her eyes, unable to look away. "Oh?"

"I'll only accept on one condition." He moved even closer and wrapped his arms around her waist.

Oh, it felt so good to finally have her in his arms again!

"Give me a second chance at our first date," he murmured. "Please. That's all I want."

Ruby shivered and lowered her lashes demurely. "Yes, I would love to go on a date with you, Brandon, but I have a condition, too."

"Go on," he pressed. Whatever she asked would be worth it. Nothing was too great a price to pay if it meant getting a second chance at their forever.

"I don't want to take anything back," she whispered against his cheek. "No redos. No starting over. Just going forward, you and me together."

"Well, I think that can be arranged," he said with a playful growl, aligning his face with hers—moving closer, closer, but still not close enough. "Can I kiss you now?" he asked.

18

*R*uby quivered when Brandon finally closed the little distance that remained between them and pressed a soft kiss to her lips.

"I had to do at least that. Otherwise, I'd be thinking about it all night," he told her with the lopsided grin she had sorely missed during his absence.

"Not exactly workplace appropriate, but I guess it's okay, seeing as I'm the boss here." Ruby giggled, then stole a second kiss. This one a bit longer, but still not quite satisfying enough. Her happiness bubbled over, standing there with him, knowing he wouldn't be leaving her behind again.

Brandon rested his chin on the top of her head, and his voice reverberated through her as he spoke.

"Do you need more time to work? If so, I can pick you up later tonight, and we can—"

"No way," she exclaimed. "You are not leaving here without me. I've been waiting for so long."

He laughed and held her even tighter. "I was hoping you'd say that."

They both let out a happy sigh as they stood holding one another for a few wordless moments.

Brandon was the one who ended the tender moment when he said, "Let me make a few quick calls out in the hall, then it's you and me—and Diamond, of course—for the rest of the evening."

Ruby felt as if she were drifting on a cloud as she floated back over to her work desk and shut down her laptop. Finally. Finally! Brandon was back in her life, and nothing could screw things up for them now.

At least she hoped that was right, given that she'd reacted too quickly, too definitively, the last time they'd run into trouble. Back then, she didn't yet know how much she'd be giving up. For as much as she'd liked Brandon then, his extended absence really had made her heart grow fonder. Cliché or not, she now knew how her life looked without him in it—and she'd hated it.

This time Brandon knocked before pushing the

main door open. "Are you two ready?" he asked, tucking his phone into his suit jacket pocket.

"I feel really underdressed compared to you," she admitted, looking over his perfectly tailored suit and crisp shirt and tie. "Maybe we should stop by my place real quick so I can change."

Brandon smiled as he shook his head. "I figured you might say that, and while I think you look beautiful exactly as you are, I may have called in a favor from a friend." He headed back into the hallway and returned with a garment bag, which he promptly handed to Ruby.

"Taking a big risk, aren't you? Buying clothes for a fashion designer."

"Maybe," he answered in a sing-song voice. "But I have a feeling you'll like what I picked out for you."

Ruby carefully unzipped the bag to reveal a stunning red gown. "Is this...?" She let her words trail off as she freed the garment the rest of the way.

"Yours? Yes, it is." He took the dress and held it up so she could take in the full view.

"Whoa," Ruby said on a slow exhale. "It's the one I designed for Millie Sullivan to wear to this year's Academy Awards. How did you get this?"

"Like I said, I called in a favor from a friend. I just

didn't mention that it was *your* friend. Millie sends her regards, by the way."

"This is the dress that changed everything," she said wistfully, thinking back to that day. "The one that got me discovered."

"Which is why I thought it only fitting that you'd wear it tonight. I also have my stylist Florence waiting outside in case you'd like her help with hair or makeup."

Her words shook as she studied the man before her. "Where are you taking me?" It was already perfect now that they were together again. Did Brandon have something even grander planned for this evening?

"Oh, not far," he said, rocking back and forth on the heels of his feet.

She had to resist the urge to push her body close to his again. Otherwise, they'd risk ruining the lovely gown. "Keeping it a secret, are you?"

"For now, yes. But the faster you get ready, the faster you'll find out what it is," he ground out. Oh, how she loved that he was teasing her!

"Well, then, send in Florence," Ruby said with a determined glint in her eyes. "I think I'm going to need all the help I can get."

*W*hen Ruby reappeared wearing the beautiful red Oscars gown, Brandon practically had to pick his jaw up off the floor.

"What do you think?" Ruby asked, giving a little twirl. "Is red my color?"

"It's like this dress was made for you." He wanted to wrap both arms around her and stand here kissing her all night, but he also couldn't wait for her to see what he'd planned for the two of them.

"Well, it was made *by* me, and that's kind of the same thing."

"Are you ready?" Brandon asked, offering his arm in a gentlemanly fashion.

Ruby placed her hand gently on his forearm almost as if they were about to perform some beautiful dance. In a way, they were.

They mounted the stairs but instead of going down toward the street level, Brandon guided Ruby upward. She remained quiet as the two of them climbed the stairs then pushed through the thick metal door onto the rooftop terrace.

Diamond instantly spotted the basket of new

toys he'd planted to keep her busy for the evening. She ran over in a flash to work on finding a favorite.

"What is all this?" Ruby asked, stepping daintily across the cement rooftop.

Strings of softly glowing red Christmas lights had been strung about overhead even though the midday sun still hung high in the sky. Brandon had also ordered a dance floor and requested that a table for two be set up in time for their arrival. He was pleased to see that everything had arrived exactly as planned.

Ruby gasped as she took it all in. "How did all of this get up here without me noticing?"

He wrapped his arms around her from behind and placed his chin on her shoulder. "Do you like it?"

"It's wonderful," she said as he spun her to face him, then planted a kiss right in the center of her forehead.

"I ordered the dance floor so that you wouldn't have to worry about spoiling your dress on the cement. C'mon." He left her in the center of the small, polished floor, then dropped his phone into the sound system after he'd queued up the playlist he'd made for their date.

"What? No string quartet?" Ruby asked with one hand resting sassily on her hip.

Brandon closed in and circled his arms around her waist, and together they began to sway to the opening notes of John Legend's most famous ballad. "I wanted us to have a bit of privacy, since I only just got you back in my arms, and I don't want anyone to distract us from one another."

They danced and danced until the playlist looped back to the start, but still Brandon didn't want to let Ruby go.

"I suppose I should call in the chef," he said with a sigh. "Even though I'm not quite ready to share you yet."

"Brandon," she said, brushing her lips across his neck. "I'm yours and only yours for as long as you'll have me."

He smiled and looked up toward the sky. "Don't go saying things like that, or I just might keep you forever."

19

*B*randon and Ruby enjoyed a slow, leisurely meal of chateaubriand with breaded zucchini and fingerling potatoes—Brandon's favorite, now that he no longer had his father's rules to follow. By the time they finished, the sun had finally begun to set, casting a dusky haze all around the city.

"Ready for part two of tonight's festivities?" he asked, excitement blooming anew. He hoped she'd love what he planned next, because it was the best part.

"There's more?" Ruby tilted her head to the side and pursed her lips in a closed mouth smile. "How could I possibly ask for anything more than this?"

"Oh, yes. There's lots more. Let's go!" He stood

and extended a hand her way. "First another quick costume change, though."

She giggled as he pulled her along. "Where are we headed this time?"

"Uh uh. Not telling," he said as they headed down the stairs and returned to Ruby's studio.

She instantly spotted the new gown that had been draped over her workstation. "This looks like mine, too," she exclaimed fingering the beadwork.

"Your design, but my friend Vera's work," Brandon informed her with an approving smile on his face. "I remember seeing you for the first time and thinking you looked like a second-place trophy in all that silver. You're nobody's second place, which is why I asked Vera to remake this beauty in gold."

"Aww, I'm your trophy," she said, lifting her arms up and looping them around his neck.

"Mmm." He lowered his face, so that he could nuzzle his face against her neck. "I don't know what I did to win your affection, but I'm glad I did."

They swayed together again, even there was no music.

"I could stay here with you all night," Ruby murmured. Now that they were back together, she never wanted to let him go.

"No," he said, suddenly snapping out of the spell.

"We still have more to do. C'mon, my driver's waiting outside."

"Where are we...?" she started, then shook her head. "That's right. You refuse to spoil the surprise."

"This time I'm okay with cluing you in early." Brandon held the door open and waited for Ruby to pass into the hallway. "We're on our way to Times Square."

She shuddered at this revelation. "Now that's somewhere I try to avoid as much as humanly possible. Why are we headed into that swarm of tourists?"

"Because it's the most surefire place to get photographed," he revealed with a wink.

"And we want that to happen?" she asked, aghast.

They both slid into the back of the Town Car, then the driver shut the door gently behind him.

"Last time they caught us by surprise," Brandon reminded her, looping his arm over her shoulder and pulling her close and gestured toward the front of the car. "This time we're ready, and *we* control the narrative. Besides, Buckley here has a huge adventure planned for him and Diamond tonight, too."

Ruby chewed on her lip and cast her eyes downward. "But what if they...?"

"I don't care about them," he said, squeezing her

hand in his. "I only care about us, and it's better that we get this over with in the beginning. Then there will be no waiting for the other shoe to drop."

"You're right," she conceded. "So, what are we going to do once we get there?"

"Same thing we've been doing all night," he said, his eyes shining with mirth. "Dancing."

*B*randon hated saying good night to Ruby when he dropped her and Diamond off at her apartment much later that night. He loved knowing he'd see her again soon, especially considering they both lived in New York City now.

When he awoke the next morning, he found several photos of the two of them splashed across the various social media sites, just as he'd expected to happen. Some insulted Ruby; others made fun of him. But there were also a blessed few that praised the new couple and said how cute they were together.

None of this really mattered, of course, because the newest edition of *Bloom* also hit newsstands this morning, and Brandon had made sure to wake up early so that he could snag one of the very first copies. On his way to see Ruby, he picked up breakfast from her favorite small diner, too—blueberry pancakes for both of them and a side of freshly grilled sausage for Diamond.

At six thirty he arrived at Ruby's apartment carrying both items in his overfull arms. He took a deep, calming breath before pressing down hard on the buzzer.

"Brandon?" came Ruby's voice about a minute later. "It's so early," she said with a yawn, then buzzed him up without offering any further argument.

She stood waiting for him in the doorway and planted a kiss on his cheek when he joined her. "I hardly got four hours of sleep. Why are you here so early?" she asked around another yawn.

"I brought us breakfast," he said, lifting the bag demonstratively. "And this." He handed her the glossy new magazine, trying his best to control his excitement. He hadn't read the feature yet but knew it would be good.

"What's this?" Ruby asked, studying the cover. Her eyes grew wide when she spied his name in the upper right corner. *"Brandon Price on Love and Happiness. Wow."*

"You start reading while I plate up our pancakes," he said, leaving her to flip through the pages on her own until she found the interview Lorna had scored for him with the *Bloom* editor-in-chief.

When Ruby finally found the feature, she cleared her throat and began to read aloud:

"'Recently I sat down with bad boy heart-throb Brandon Price, former heir to the Body by Price empire, to discuss why he's leaving it all behind for love.'"

She paused and craned her neck, searching the tiny apartment until at last she found him watching her with a bemused smile.

"Keep reading," he urged.

She grabbed a drink from the water bottle on her coffee table and picked up where she left off:

"'My father has built an amazing company,' Price said. 'But it's his. I wanted to build something that was mine.' He then went on to describe his new business venture, Diamond Media Consulting, a consultancy that helps both new and seasoned celebs navigate the choppy waters of fame.

"'I got the idea from a very good friend of mine, fashion designer Ruby Ross. She saw this potential in me before I ever saw it in myself. I was still scared of upsetting my father, and if it weren't for Ruby, I probably never would have found the courage to get out there and find what really makes me happy. And that's Ruby. She's not just a friend, but also my hero and the love of my life.'"

Ruby lowered the magazine at the same exact time Brandon plopped down on the couch beside her. "This article used the word *love* like three times. Are you maybe trying to tell me something?"

He grabbed her hand and kissed it on both sides. "Yes, Ruby, I love you."

"Well, I already knew that. I figured it out a long time ago." Ruby giggled and placed her head on his chest, right above his heart, then looked up at him with big, searching eyes.

"I love you, too, Brandon. And I love everything that got us here."

They exchanged a slow, leisurely kiss. They didn't need to rush, because both knew they had the rest of their long lives ahead to share these blissful signs of their affection for one another.

"You know, I really do have to work," she murmured after some time. "I don't want to, but I have to."

"That's okay," he said, giving her one last peck on the lips. "Can I stop by to see you again tonight?"

"You better!" she said with a playful smile. "I'll be waiting."

But Brandon knew that they didn't have to wait anymore. They'd officially started their forever, and —oh—was it sweet!

20

*A*s Brandon left Ruby's apartment, it felt as if his entire world was now exactly as it should be. Despite the early hour, his phone buzzed in his pocket. And when he fished it out, he was surprised to see his father's number flash across the screen.

"Dad?" he asked, not bothering to hide the shock in his voice. "Isn't it like five o'clock in LA?"

He made a dismissive sound, then said, "Your mother called me about an hour ago, said I needed to see what our son has been up to."

Brandon's stomach dropped straight to the ground. If his father had called to insult him or say mean things about Ruby, he wouldn't be able to keep it cordial. Not this time. "And?" he asked, his throat suddenly very dry.

"Well, first I did a quick check on the ol' Internet, then I read the article your mother scanned and sent to me via email," he ground out slowly. "From that ladies mag, *Bloom*, I think it was."

"And?" Brandon asked again, desperate for his father's verdict even though it bore no credence in how he'd choose to live his life going forward.

His father cleared his throat. Whatever he had to say clearly wasn't coming out very easily. "And I'm proud of you, son," he said at last, his voice clear and strong. Unmistakably sincere. "I'm also sorry for the things I said before. It wasn't right of me to—"

"Dad," Brandon said, cutting his father off. "Thank you for apologizing. Do you really mean it? Because I'd love for you and Mom to meet Ruby one day."

His dad sighed, but his voice remained kind. "I didn't understand before, but now I do. She's good for you, and that makes her the most beautiful woman in all the world."

Brandon didn't care if it wasn't manly when a tear escaped his eye and rolled down his cheek. "Thank you, Dad. That means a lot."

"Well, be sure you thank Ruby for me, too. It

seems she taught you some things about being a man, and then you turned right around and showed them to me."

"I will, Dad," he promised, his voice shaky as he found himself overcome with emotions—each and every one of them positive.

"One more question before we say goodbye," his dad said.

"Yeah?" Brandon still couldn't believe his entire life had changed in less than twenty-four hours, and that his hard work had been the catalyst.

"Would it be possible for me to hire Diamond Media Consulting?" his dad asked with a chuckle. "I hear they have some pretty good ideas over there."

"Well then, Mr. Price, it looks like I'm hired," Brandon said, ushering in yet another new era—this time for he and his father.

To think, just months ago he'd assumed that he would never find his way into a new, happier life. But then he'd met a beautiful woman, and everything changed for the better.

SNEAK PEEK

Read the first chapter of DIGGING THE DRIVER, book 2 of the Celebrity Corgi Romances...

"*N*ow turn toward me, hands on your hips. That's it. A gentle smile. Now tip your head back just a little more. Perfect. Let your hair cascade down your back. Look right at the camera. Perfect."

Lissa did as she was instructed, but only because she'd learned long ago just to cooperate. It was the easiest way to get these photo sessions over with and the hordes of people surrounding her to vanish.

"One last shot, and we can call it quits. Left hand up over your head and angled back down. Turn your right shoulder inward a little more. Let's see you flirt a little with the camera, like you would with a new man in your life." *New man?* It was the last thing she wanted. The only thing she needed was her sweet corgi, Bella. Now that was a relationship she could trust.

Images of Bella at the rescue shelter looking lost and afraid still had the power to make Lissa's heart ache. Poor thing must have been the runt of the litter because she was small for a corgi. Add to that not being fed very well, and she'd been downright bony. It had been a spur-of-the-moment decision to get a pet of her own finally. Growing up, she'd often visited the shelter in Bellevue, a small bedroom community just outside of Charlotte, and had helped out whenever she could. Every animal in the place deserved a loving home. It broke her heart each time she'd left, their sad and confused faces calling to her to do something more for them.

Adopting Bella was the smartest decision she ever made. Lissa had gone looking for a pet, but what she'd found was much better. She'd found a best friend. It was also the day she started working at the rescue shelter regularly, hoping to make a difference for so many other animals who deserved more than to be homeless.

She hadn't seen the direction her help would take at the time, but she was pleased with the inroads of success being made over the past four years.

"This isn't working. You look like you've lost your best friend, not excited about finding a new one with potential." Emily King, the photographer from *Bloom* magazine, stopped taking pictures, her mouth in a tight line. "Remember, this is *Blossom*, your signature scent. A scent that empowers women to not only feel beautiful but to take on the world with power and confidence. A scent to inspire woman to greater heights."

"Sorry. I'm a little tired." *Tired of being photographed*—one of the top three things she hated about her celebrity driver status.

"Okay, try this. Imagine you're looking at a new stock car just delivered, and you're ready to slide into the driver's seat and test out the way it handles on the racetrack for the first time."

A sweet image for sure. The clicking whirr of the camera was a good sign.

"That's it. Beautiful." Emily lowered her camera and smiled. "And that's a wrap."

Thank goodness.

"Sorry, Emily. Sometimes, it's hard to get into the right frame of mind for something like this."

"No worries. Trust me, I get all kinds of scenarios when it comes to bringing out the best in my subjects. You're one of the easy ones." Emily laughed.

"That's good to hear. Will you be coming to the Walker Charity Gala on June 1st?"

"I'm going to try and make it, but I have some scheduling conflicts. I heard Ruby Ross and a few others from *Bloom* are going."

"Yes. It'll be great to see Ruby again."

"You two knew each other before the *Bloom* magazine connection, didn't you?"

"We met in college, but we didn't actually connect back then." Ruby was one of those women that surprised you once you got to know them. Or maybe the problem was Lissa's. Unfortunately, she hadn't given the woman a chance back then.

"Funny how life brings people back into your life for a second chance." Emily laughed, tucking her camera into the hard-shell case.

"True." Ruby was a powerhouse in the fashion industry, and they had become friends at the extravagant parties *Bloom* magazine threw each year. Lissa had been honored to be invited to attend Ruby's recent wedding to Brandon Price, one of the sexiest men alive according to People's Magazine Sexiest 25. The reception party had been touted in every magazine for month's and was easily considered the "in" wedding of the year.

Marriage wasn't in the cards for Lissa, but it was nice to see those around her happy.

"It looks like everyone's almost got everything cleaned up in here. I should probably get a move on. It was great to see you again."

"You, too." Lissa watched as Emily followed the rest of her crew down the hall to leave.

Bev, her friend and marketing manager, and one of the few people she truly trusted, was deep in conversation with one of the set assistants. During the photoshoot, Bev had stood on the sidelines with Bella, watching the progress.

She'd met Bev Masters when she'd first come onto the racing scene five years ago, and they'd become friends. Bev was in marketing, and when she'd gotten wind Lissa had entered the pole event for what is considered the longest and most grueling stock car race at the Charlotte Motor Speedway, she'd gone out of her way to contrive a meeting. It wasn't often a woman took on the challenge of the racing against the biggest names in the business, especially for her debut race. It had taken a bit of fancy footwork on Bev's part, but in the end, Lissa was glad she'd given the woman a chance to prove herself.

The celebrity endorsements that came with competing in a man's world required a full-time person to manage. Over time, Bev had earned her trust—something Lissa didn't give out easily. After her parents' success in the video world, she'd learned the hard way that trust wasn't a five-letter word, it was four. L-I-E-S.

Bev was different from the other people who wanted her attention, and now Lissa wasn't sure what she would do without her. The picture of smooth efficiency, the woman always looked like she'd stepped straight out of a magazine with every-thing effortlessly in place, unlike the hours it took Lissa to transform herself from her usual never-ready harried look. Her friend understood her better than anyone, including her need to race cars.

Racing was the ultimate in control, something Lissa craved after having spent years on the sidelines at first by choice, and then later as the result of her parents' video gaming success catapulting her into a world she didn't understand. A world where people thought nothing of using someone to get what they wanted. A world she hated.

The crew soon left, and finally, the house was back to the peace and quiet Lissa enjoyed.

"I'm glad that's over." Lissa glanced at her watch. "Travis Howard from SDS should be here soon for our appointment." Yet another interruption to her solitude, but this one had a more far-reaching impact.

"Thank goodness." Bev offered her a light cardigan.

Lissa slid it over her bare shoulders to cover the satiny material of the halter top that left her chilled. The top had been the art director at *Bloom* magazine's choice for Lissa's signature fragrance advertisement. Neither Lissa nor Bev had control when it came to these photo shoots if they stayed within the preset guidelines—nothing scanty or provocative.

She wasn't exactly model material, and her well-developed, muscular arms and solidly built frame were accentuated instead of hidden. Something she'd tried to do most of her life.

Lissa had learned first-hand how catty and mean people could be from jealousy, wanting what she had and not understanding how hard she worked to get where she was on the racing circuit.

"We've talked about this and I'm sorry. But there's a lot going on the next few weeks, and I can't always babysit Bella. Not that I mind, you understand, it's just sometimes it makes my job impossible." Bev handed Bella to Lissa.

Bella bombed her face with doggie kisses from a wet tongue, and Lissa rubbed her cheek dry. Her baby was spoiled but too darn cute to resist. Bella had the airs and grace of a princess, and over the years, she'd insisted on being treated like one. When Lissa had first brought her home, she'd barely weighed in at ten pounds and carrying her around had been easy, but at twenty-two pounds now, it was a different story. Lissa didn't have the heart to say no when she yipped to be held, and truth be told, she enjoyed being needed by her canine companion.

"I understand. It stinks we even need to worry about a dognapper, but yesterday's dognapping makes eleven in the Charlotte vicinity. The dogs are all purebreds, but there have been no ransom notes yet. I can't stand the thought of Bella being taken by these unsavory characters for who knows what purpose." Lissa had been toying with the idea of security for Bella because she wasn't always in a position to keep her safe. Yesterday's incident was the final straw that prompted the call to South Division Securities. SDS came highly recommended, and when she found out Travis Williams worked there, it had been a no-brainer to use the company.

The only downside being that he was her former best friend's cousin. The three of them had been close back in high school, at least they were until her world had been turned upside down by her parents' success. She'd always wondered what happened to Damien, but it was easier not to think of him or the way he'd hurt her. Travis on the other hand, was still a friend, one she ran into occasionally in town. He would be a hundred times better than dealing with a stranger, especially considering he would be temporarily be living in her home.

"I know. I just wish the police would catch these criminals and put an end to the fear these dognappings have created in everyone's hearts. I can't even begin to imagine what these pet owners feel having their babies stolen."

Lissa snuggled Bella close and kissed the top of her head. "The photographers are gone, baby girl. And don't you worry, Mommy's going to keep you safe from those bad guys." She sat down on the sofa and leaned back; Bella happily situated against her chest.

"Bella's not a real baby, you know." Bev laughed.

"She is to me." Lissa nuzzled up against Bella's cheek, loving the feel of her silky fur if you brushed it in the right direction.

"Technically, she's forty-two years old in people years." Bev moved to the side table and poured herself a glass of wine. "Want one?" She nodded her head to indicate the wine.

"Sure. It might help relax me for this next appointment. Forty-two or otherwise, what dog doesn't love to be pampered?" Lissa smiled. She put Bella down on the floor and accepted the glass of wine, eager for a moment to relax. Bella took off down the hall, probably in search of one of her toys.

"Bella has you wrapped."

"Probably, but I like it. You know, I've mentioned it before, but I'd like to start doing less and less of these endorsements. They're just not me." She took a sip of wine, enjoying the crisp sauvignon blanc.

"They may not be you, but they are part of your image. An image that pays back when it comes to marketing. You're living in a man's world, and there's big money in the fact that you're all woman. Something I'm sure none of the male drivers can forget."

"Which isn't necessarily a good thing. Some of them can be downright insulting, their egos are not quite up to a little feminine competition."

"True." Bev smiled. "I'll see what I can do to cut back on your commitments, but we need to get through the ones scheduled already. Things are ramped up right now with the second annual Walker Rescue Shelter Gala coming up. You know, the one you personally endorse."

"I hear you. And for the rescue dogs, I'll put up with anything, but then you already knew that."

"I do. Don't forget we need to be at the Taylors' pre-gala cocktail party by seven-thirty tonight. There will be some big names, and hopefully some big donations. The Taylors are counting on you."

Lissa let out a frustrated sigh. It would have been nice just relax the rest of the evening, considering she had practice time scheduled on the track in the morning. Traveling at speeds of over two hundred miles per hour was dangerous, doing it at less than one hundred percent focus could be deadly.

"I'll be ready." Somehow, she'd have to get through the party and get a good night's sleep, something made even less likely with Travis sleeping under her roof for the near future. She hadn't seen him in years, and it would take some getting used to the idea of having a security detail around twenty-four-seven for Bella.

*D*amien drove down Sunset River Way, shaking his head at the showy estates in the gated community, each one grandiose in its own way. These people had plenty of the almighty dollar, but no kids were playing in the yard, no toys left out haphazardly, or animals running loose. Instead, everything here was coldly impersonal and meticulously cared for. The old adage about money not buying happiness came to mind.

Of course, this is where Lissa Walker lived. He'd expected nothing less from the famous Walkers and their spoiled daughter. He was, however, surprised she'd even stayed in Bellevue. He'd pegged her and Tony Carruthers as two people this little town could never satisfy. Of course, it was no more surprising than when he'd found out she was competing on a professional level at the Charlotte Motor Speedway in the Coca-Cola 600.

On the other hand, Tony, Bellevue High's super-star, super stud, and super jerk, had left right after high school to play college football. He'd never made it as a professional player, which didn't hurt Damien's feelings one bit.

Damien used to enjoy football and racing, but

between Lissa and Tony, they'd manage to ruin both sports for him. Mr. King and Queen of the senior prom were welcome to whatever they got in life. Damien was just glad he'd discovered the real Lissa Walker before he'd spilled his guts to her about his feelings.

He pulled into the driveway and entered the gate code his cousin had given him. Travis had a legitimate reason he couldn't be at the appointment he'd scheduled. Damien, on the other hand, had a legitimate reason *not* to want to be here. *Lissa.*

Damien shook his head as he surveyed the manicured lawn and bushes. It was late spring, and most lawns were just starting to turn green, but hers, like every other house in this neighborhood, were bright green and would have been for months. Overseeded with rye, most likely by a professional gardener. Nothing but the best for a Walker.

The house—correction, make that the mansion —was built of stone and stood three stories high. The widow's walk at the top would provide an unparalleled view of the Catawba River and the countryside.

He'd give anything to be back at the office reviewing his most recent client's corporate files. Figuring out who was hacking into their computers was far more appealing than covering for his cousin, but family was important to him.

Saying no to Travis was never really an option, not after what his family had done for Damien's family. Travis's mother had them all in and helped them weather through the worst of times after the media storm that ruined Damien's parents' lives. A storm filled with sensationalism and lies, but no one cared when the truth finally came out—by then it was old news. All except for the family they destroyed in the process.

Damien slid out of the jeep and made his way to the porch. A little tan, white, and black dog came through the open front door and started to bark. Damien chuckled, hoping the dog had more bark than bite. It was a funny-looking, squat thing with the shortest legs he'd ever seen on a dog.

He looked around but didn't see anyone nearby. The dog continued to bark, doing a miniature show of charge and retreat, as if unsure how brave he wanted to be. Damien knelt to let the cute little fellow smell his hand. The dog inched his way closer and the barking stopped.

Damien stroked his back lightly. "Hey there, little guy. What are you doing out here?"

The dog couldn't answer, of course, but talking

was all Damien could think of to do to calm the dog enough so he could pick him up and take him back inside without biting off his hand. Damien's experience with dogs amounted to zero, but leaving him outside wasn't an option, just in case he'd escaped.

Damien picked up the dog, a little surprised he didn't seem to mind. He stepped up on the porch and knocked, pushing the door open at the same time. He took one tentative step inside, glancing down the hall. "Hello? Anyone home?" He spotted someone coming toward him.

"Hey there, who are you? That's my dog! Put her down!" *Lissa Walker in the flesh.* The suddenness of coming face-to-face with her slowed the function of his brain and his ability to respond.

"Bev, call the police!" Lissa hollered.

Police? "Whoa! Hold up a minute." He held up his free hand. "There's no need for the police. Your front door was open, and I did knock. Your dog was outside. I thought I was doing you a favor by bringing him back inside to keep him from running away." So much for being cool and reserved. He'd never had the police called on him before, and he didn't intend to start now.

"Damien?" The word was filled with derision, and her face scrunched up as if his name tasted like bile. But then he hadn't expected a warm welcome. Their history didn't exactly spell happy reunion.

He handed Bella to Lissa. "It's nice to know you remember me." Especially since he hadn't forgotten her—not that he hadn't tried. But with her face plastered on every racing magazine, not to mention several others that lined the shelves at the grocery store checkouts, it wasn't like he could forget.

Seeing her in magazines had done nothing to prepare him for the up-close-and-personal view he had now. Beautiful, poised, and in control. Her sapphire-blue eyes were filled with icy scorn. Her dark-brown hair, once short and fluffy, fell in long gorgeous tresses across her shoulders. An urge to smooth back the loose tendrils from her cheek threatened to overwhelm him, but he held it in check. He despised the male appreciation he couldn't seem to control.

"Thank you." The words seemed dragged from her lips. "For your information, the photoshoot crew just left, and they must have left the door open. It's not an invitation to walk into someone's home. What are you doing here?"

"I'm with SDS. Travis had a family emergency and asked me to fill in for him. I understand you need security."

"I do. Or I did. Not with you." She stood feet apart, one hand clutching the dog, the other wrapped protectively around the animal as she rubbed behind her ears.

"Suit yourself. I wasn't keen on this job myself." At least there was one thing they could agree upon. Damien turned to leave.

"Wait a minute. What's going on here?" Another voice made Damien hesitate and turn back.

A woman had joined them, pushing her glasses back on her nose to get a better look at him. She was the epitome of efficiency, and her tone demanded answers.

"He's with SDS. Travis can't make it and thought it would be okay to send Damien. It's not. Okay, that is." Lissa huffed.

"Damien?" The woman looked him over from head to toe, the look of appreciation in her eyes all too obvious.

"Damien Trent, to be exact. An old, let's say, ex-friend, from high school."

The woman looked back and forth between him and Lissa. She shook her head. "What does it matter who provides the security? What matters is that you have it. You know how important it is, Lissa."

"I am standing here, ladies. So, what's it going to

be? Do you need a bodyguard or not? Or is this just another celebrity ploy to show off your popularity and wealth?"

Damien didn't like the sudden smirk that turned Lissa's thin-lined lips upward ever so slightly. The feeling of unease grew when she shot the other woman a quick look and shook her head. Secret code for don't say a word. He'd seen the look time and time again in his business, and it was never good.

"I do need security. You say you're filling in for Travis?" Her grinned widened.

"I am. Just for a few days." Lissa was up to no good. One minute she was ready to call the police, and the next she seemed all too happy to let him take over Travis's contract.

"Travis signed on for full-time. Our deal was for him to stay on for as long as I felt extra security was needed. Are you prepared for that?" The dog nudged her hand to continue the rubbing when Lissa stopped.

"That's fine. Is there any reason you've suddenly become gung-ho for security that I should know about? Travis didn't provide me with very many details. I thought I could get those from you." The truth was Damien hadn't given his cousin much chance to explain once he'd found out the name of the client.

"There have been no threats if that's what you're asking. I just want precautionary security."

"It's always been about you, hasn't it? At least it has been ever since your parents came out with their Dark Dragon Hunter videogame." The sarcasm in his voice couldn't be helped. Not after all these years.

"You have no idea what you're talking about. But back in high school, you didn't stick around long enough to find out. Let's just hope when the going gets tough working for me, you don't run away again." She bit down on the side of her lower lip as if to keep from saying anything else. If she bit it any harder, she'd soon draw blood.

"I'm only here until Travis can take back over his own assignment. There's not much I can't handle, so don't worry. I've got you covered. The contract terms call for the arrangement to start in the morning and I'll be here first thing." At least it would give him the night to readjust to what the next few days would be like because seeing her in person was a whole lot harder than dealing with the memory.

"What? Travis knew I had a cocktail party to attend tonight. We talked about it and he agreed to cover for me tonight."

"She's right. He did agree. Surely you can cancel your plans for the evening. This is important to Lissa." The woman was quick to jump in and try to help sway his decision. Two against one but it wouldn't work.

"Travis said nothing about starting tonight and I have a prior engagement. This was supposed to be just a precursor meeting to iron out some of the details. Sorry ladies, but I really can't stay." Damien nodded his head and turned to leave.

"But what am I supposed to do with Bella?" Lissa spoke up, stopping him as he reached for the doorknob.

He glanced back. "Bella?"

Lissa started down the hall toward him. "My dog." She pointed at the corgi still safely ensconced in her arms.

"How should I know? I'm not exactly a dog person, but I would think whatever you normally do with her."

"That's why I hired SDS. I can't do what I normally do, not with the dognappers still on the loose."

"What does SDS have to do with Bella?" Damien was totally confused at this point, but an uneasy feeling settled in the pit of his stomach.

"You're her guard. You know, your job. Bella's new doggy guard." Her words sunk in like a kick to the solar plexus.

"I agreed to nothing of the sort. Travis indicated you needed security, a bodyguard. I'm not babysitting a dog. Check her into doggy daycare or something like that—like normal people do. Have a good evening, ladies."

The sparkle in Lissa's eyes was a telltale sign she'd known he didn't have a clue as to the true purpose of why SDS had been hired, and she'd enjoyed dropping the bomb. It explained the secret the two women had shared earlier. He shouldn't have expected anything less from Lissa, but it didn't change anything. He wasn't babysitting a dog.

"So you're running away? Again. You haven't changed much, have you? How will it look for SDS when you renege on a contract? Because you can be sure everyone will find out. Bella needs protection, and the way I see it, you don't have a choice. Unless Travis has some other underling, one he can force to take his place for a few days. Bella means everything to me, and that means putting up with having security people around, even if it's you." Her threat landed its mark. Backed into a corner, he didn't have much choice.

"Fine. First thing in the morning, I'll be here. Seven a.m. sharp. It's only for a couple of days. And for the record, the dislike you have for me, it's mutual. It'll make things easier with us being on the same page."

Want to keep reading? Head to https://
sweetpromisepress.com/CelebrityCorgi to grab your
copy now!

What's our Sweet Promise? It's to deliver the heart-warming, entertaining, clean, and wholesome reads you love with every single book.

From contemporary to historical romances to suspense and even cozy mysteries, all of our books are guaranteed to put a song in your heart and a smile on your face. That's our promise to you, and we can't wait to deliver upon it...

We release one new book per week, which means the flow of sweet, relatable reads coming your way never ends. Make sure to save some space on your eReader!

Check out our books in Kindle Unlimited at
sweetpromisepress.com/Unlimited

Download our free app to keep up with the latest
releases and unlock cool bonus content at
sweetpromisepress.com/App

Join our reader discussion group, meet our authors,
and make new friends at
sweetpromisepress.com/Group

Sign up for our weekly newsletter at
sweetpromisepress.com/Subscribe

And don't forget to like us on Facebook at
sweetpromisepress.com/FB

*Meet six Corgis who live the high life as celebrity BFFs.
One thing's for sure: When their people fall in love, it
better be with someone who loves dogs as much as
they do!*

FLIRTING WITH THE FASHIONISTA BY MELISSA STORM

Ruby Ross is the rising star plus-sized fashion since she's just signed the deal of a lifetime for a new line of retail shops across the country. Now she and her faithful corgi, Diamond, are constantly on the go overseeing the production of her franchises and getting to know all the must-meets of the fashion and beauty world.

As the heir to his father's enormous fitness and

supplement empire, Brandon Price is constantly in the public eye. Assigning him to serve as the face of the brand, nobody ever asked what Brandon wanted out of life. And Brandon never knew either... until he set eyes on the big, beautiful powerhouse, Ruby Ross. She stands for everything his father hates, which makes him crave her that much more.

But Ruby has way too much to do to make time for idle flirtations. Besides surviving high school as a bigger girl has her a little gun shy when it comes to romance—and especially to pretty boys like Brandon. With the help of a mischievous, little Corgi, can these two put their differences aside to find love is much more than skin deep?

DIGGING THE DRIVER BY ELSIE DAVIS

As a professional race car driver, Lissa Walker is used to dealing with all sorts of threats. But when a dognapper starts targeting her hometown, she'll do anything to protect her corgi Bella—refusing to take chances. Even if that means hiring Damien Trent, an arrogant, too-smart-for-his-own-good know-it-all.

Who also happens to be the one who broke her heart so many years ago.

Damien isn't too thrilled about taking a job that would require him to work in close quarters with Lissa, let alone one that would require him to be a doggy bodyguard. Unfortunately, for the sake of his company's reputation, he has no choice but to stick it out.

The history between the two provides much more friction than any race track ever could, but they'll have to put their past differences aside to keep little Bella safe. Everything else--including the new feelings surging between them--will just have to wait. Can they take it slow and steady when both are so tempted to zoom full-speed ahead?

ROMANCING THE ROYAL BY LAURA ASHWOOD

Emmie Walker never wanted to be a royal canine companion for the Crown corgi of Avington, but she needs some way to pay the bills until her dream of opening her own service dog training facility can become a reality. Now the best chance of making that happen is to spend the better part of her time looking after the spoiled royal corgi, Gatsby.

Gatsby, however, comes with strings attached. Namely a leash that leads right to the Prince of Avington, Dorian Tennesley. Prince Dorian leads what appears to be an enviable life, but behind his stately façade lies a man who longs for more than mere pomp and circumstance.

When the unlikely trio heads to America for a taste of real adventure, Emmie and Dorian find they have more in common than either could have ever imagined. With the help of Gatsby, might these two find themselves falling head over heels despite what it could cost them both?

CHARMING THE CHEF BY C.A. PHIPPS

Culinary student Lyra St. Claire can't believe her luck when she becomes the face of America's hottest new cooking show and an overnight sensation. For now, she's loving the lime light and with her faithful corgi, Cinnamon, by her side she knows she's on the cusp of achieving everything she's ever dreamed of.

Kaden Hunter trained side-by-side with Lyra.

While they once had a rock-solid friendship, he found himself left behind when she became a household name. Now, rising from the ashes of their one-time friendship, he's determined to make it big —no golden ticket required.

When Lyra's newest contract forces her to face her former friend turned rival, she can see all of her dreams burning up right before her. Can she and Kaden move past the bitter taste of their ruined friendship? And could the heat in the kitchen lead to something even more?

PINING FOR THE PHOTOGRAPHER BY DEBBIE WHITE

Emily King has worked hard to become the go-to photographer to the stars, but between readying her new studio and organizing an upcoming charity event, she has little time left for anything else. Well, at least her sweet corgi, Daisy, gives her all the companionship she needs. That is, until a blast from Emily's past blows right into Tinsel Town...

Stage actor Connor Stone couldn't wait to trade in the cold winters of New York City for the sunny skies of Los Angeles. And this cross-country move becomes even more of a no-brainer when he finds out his ex needs some extra hands to help prepare the charity event of the season. With his first big movie role and the one who got away both in his sites, Connor can hardly believe how close he's come to truly having it all.

But will Emily even want to make the time to get to know him again? And will she like what she sees on the other side of her camera lens? Or is their relationship best left in the archives?

DATING THE DIRECTOR BY VICTORIA BARBOUR

Acclaimed film director Millie Sullivan's newest project is a sure bet to take her from a simple nominee to a full-fledged Oscar winner. The only thing standing in her way is casting the lead part. It's perfect for her nemesis, Chris Ryan, but the secret Millie carries about the actor and his dog makes him her last choice for the role.

Chris Ryan is one of Hollywood's hottest actors. Between premier roles portraying heroes who save the day while falling in love and Skipper, his steadfast Corgi pal, women everywhere adore him. Well, except for Millie Sullivan, that is. Acting in one of Millie's films can help Chris break free from being typecast in hunky hero or rom-com darling roles, but first he needs to find out why she hates him so much.

Can Skipper help his human bestie land the role of a lifetime while also helping Millie find the will to forgive them of whatever caused her to harbor a grudge for all these years? Or is teaching these two humans to travel from enemies to lovers a trick too impossible for even the cleverest of corgis?

MORE FROM MELISSA STORM

Sign up for free stories, fun updates, and uplifting messages from Melissa at www.MelStorm.com/gift

* * *

The Church Dogs of Charleston

A very special litter of Chihuahua puppies born on Christmas day is adopted by the local church and immediately set to work as tiny therapy dogs.

Little Loves

Mini Miracles

Dainty Darlings

* * *

The Sled Dog Series

Get ready to fall in love with a special pack of working and retired sled dogs, each of whom change their new owners' lives for the better.

Let There Be Love

Let There Be Light

Let There Be Life

Season of Mercy

* * *

The First Street Church Romances

Sweet and wholesome small town love stories with the community church at their center make for the perfect feel-good reads!

Love's Prayer

Love's Promise

Love's Prophet

Love's Vow

Love's Trial

* * *

The Memory Ranch Romances

This new Sled Dogs-spinoff series harnesses the restorative power of both horses and love at Elizabeth Jane's therapeutic memory ranch.

Memories of Home

Memories of Heaven

Memories of Healing

* * *

Sweet Promise Press

What's our Sweet Promise? It's to deliver the heartwarming, entertaining, clean, and wholesome reads you love with every single book.

Saving Sarah

Flirting with the Fashionista

* * *

Stand-Alone Novels and Novellas

Whether climbing ladders in the corporate world or taking care of things at home, every woman has a story to tell.

A Mother's Love

A Colorful Life

Love & War

* * *

Special Collections & Boxed Sets

From light-hearted comedies to stories about finding hope in the darkest of times, these special boxed editions offer a great way to catch up or to fall in love with Melissa Storm's books for the first time.

The Sled Dog Series: Books 1-3

The First Street Church Romances: Books 1-3

The Church Dogs of Charleston: Books 1-3

The Alaska Sunrise Romances: Books 1-9

Finding Mr. Happily Ever After: Books 1-5

ABOUT THE AUTHOR

Melissa Storm is a mother first, and everything else second. Writing is her way of showing her daughter just how beautiful life can be, when you pay attention to the everyday wonders that surround us. So, of course, Melissa's USA Today bestselling fiction is highly personal and often based on true stories.

Melissa loves books so much, she married fellow author Falcon Storm. Between the two of them, there are always plenty of imaginative, awe-inspiring stories to share. Melissa and Falcon also run a number of book-related businesses together, including LitRing, Sweet Promise Press, Novel Publicity, Your Author Engine, and the Author Site. When she's not reading, writing, or child-rearing, Melissa spends time relaxing at home in the company of a seemingly unending quantity of dogs and a rescue cat named Schrödinger.

GET IN TOUCH!

www.MelStorm.com

author@melstorm.com

56051196R00130

Made in the USA
Middletown, DE
22 July 2019